TOUCH___

After luncheon Sir Thomas persuaded Justina to take another turn around the deck with him.

When she told him that no engagement could be announced until he had applied to her father for her hand in marriage, he was not pleased.

"This is preposterous," he exclaimed. "You are mine and I want the whole world and certainly this ship to know about it."

"My father would never countenance such a way of proceeding," responded Justina firmly.

If only she could stave off an official announcement of their engagement, there was the faint possibility that Sir Thomas might find someone else more to his liking.

Sir Thomas's face darkened suddenly.

"Who has told you our engagement should not be immediately announced," he snorted and caught hold of her arm in his strong grip.

Justina gasped in pain.

"You are hurting me," she protested.

A couple of passengers were approaching and he immediately released her.

"I am sorry, but I need you to answer my question. Who told you to say our engagement should not be announced immediately? And don't tell me it was Mrs. Arbuthnot."

"No, indeed, it was *I* who said it to *her*. Though why you should be so convinced it was her, I do not understand. After all, she is my chaperone. You cannot think," she went on, becoming indignant, "that any well brought up girl would announce that she was engaged *before* her father had given his consent?"

THE BARBARA CARTLAND PINK COLLECTION

Titles in this series

TOUCHING THE STARS

BARBARA CARTLAND

Barbaracartland.com Ltd

THE BARBARA CARTLAND PINK COLLECTION

Barbara .Cartland was the most prolific bestselling author in the history of the world. She was frequently in the Guinness Book of Records for writing more books in a year than any other living author. In fact her most amazing literary feat was when her publishers asked for more Barbara Cartland romances, she doubled her output from 10 books a year to over 20 books a year, when she was 77.

She went on writing continuously at this rate for 20 years and wrote her last book at the age of 97, thus completing 400 books between the ages of 77 and 97.

Her publishers finally could not keep up with this phenomenal output, so at her death she left 160 unpublished manuscripts, something again that no other author has ever achieved.

Now the exciting news is that these 160 original unpublished Barbara Cartland books are already being published and by Barbaracartland.com exclusively on the internet, as the international web is the best possible way of reaching so many Barbara Cartland readers around the world.

The 160 books are published monthly and will be numbered in sequence.

The series is called the Pink Collection as a tribute to Barbara Cartland whose favourite colour was pink and it became very much her trademark over the years.

The Barbara Cartland Pink Collection is published only on the internet. Log on to www.barbaracartland.com to find out how you can purchase the books monthly as they are published, and take out a subscription that will ensure that all subsequent editions are delivered to you by mail order to your home.

NEW

Barbaracartland.com is proud to announce the publication of ten new Audio Books for the first time as CDs. They are favourite Barbara Cartland stories read by well-known actors and actresses and each story extends to 4 or 5 CDs. The Audio Books are as follows :

The Patient Bridegroom	The Passion and the Flower
A Challenge of Hearts	Little White Doves of Love
A Train to Love	The Prince and the Pekinese
The Unbroken Dream	A King in Love
The Cruel Count	A Sign of Love

More Audio Books will be published in the future and the above titles can be purchased by logging on to the website www.barbaracartland.com or please write to the address below.

If you do not have access to a computer, you can write for information about the Barbara Cartland Pink Collection and the Barbara Cartland Audio Books to the following address :

Barbara Cartland.com Ltd.
Camfield Place,
Hatfield,
Hertfordshire AL9 6JE
United Kingdom.
Telephone: +44 (0)1707 642629
Fax: +44 (0)1707 663041

CHAPTER ONE
1894

Justina Mansell arranged her small stool on the edge of the wood. Carefully, she unpacked her watercolours and painting implements.

She sighed with pleasure as she sat down and gazed at the scene laid out before her.

The bluebells had never looked better. They spread from her feet out into the distance, their blue set off by the fresh green of the undergrowth and the trees.

In fact, as she studied the bluebells, she thought that they reflected the sadness that lay below her appreciation of their beauty.

Justina had wanted to accompany her mother to her favourite charity, the local hospital. Lady Mansell spent a good amount of time visiting and raising money for it.

She had smiled and placed her hand on Justina's cheek.

"No, my darling, you go and enjoy yourself."

Justina knew it was hopeless to try and persuade her mother. Lady Mansell always did exactly what she wanted.

The fact that what she wanted was usually to help others rather than to enjoy herself with her family did not make it any easier for her youngest daughter to accept.

It made Justina feel useless and that there was no purpose to her life.

Justina felt a failure.

She had failed as a *debutante*.

The previous year she had come out with a Season sponsored by her aunt, the Viscountess Elder of Bannockburn, her father's sister. The whole purpose behind the Season, she knew, had been to find a husband.

It had not been a success.

Justina had been bored with the company of the other *debutantes*, none of whom seemed to have a thought in their heads beyond their appearance and the necessity of making a suitable marriage.

And none of the young men had shown the slightest interest in her.

It was useless to recall that she had not been interested in any of them either.

A second failure was Justina's inability to make a life for herself in Surrey.

Croquet parties, picnics and supper parties with their neighbours she found boring. Nothing new ever happened and nobody seemed able to talk about anything interesting.

And too often both Lady and Lord Mansell said something that betrayed they were waiting for Justina to find a husband.

Were all young men as dull as those she had so far met? Why could not they be like her father?

When Lord Mansell was home, he would regale her with stories of life at the Foreign Office and what was happening in the outside world. Talking to him was fascinating.

Then there was Justina's brother, Peter, a soldier and now serving with his Regiment in India. She used to enjoy talking to him.

Her latest failure seemed to be as a companion to her mother, a role that Justina had assumed herself. But whenever Justina suggested she accompanied or helped her, Lady Mansell said she should go and enjoy herself with friends of her own age.

There were only two activities that Justina felt she was successful at – playing the piano and painting.

Both could carry her away into another world.

She tried to concentrate on colours in the vegetation all around her.

Painting was an occupation that never disappointed Justina. Trying to capture a flower in all its incredible beauty was something that could make her forget all the frustrations of everyday life.

Her mother would laugh and say,

"If an earthquake should happen while Justina is painting, she would not notice!"

Justina certainly did not now hear her sister, Victoria, calling her name or see her running across the field that led to the wood, waving a letter.

Only when Victoria arrived at her side and put a hand on her shoulder, trying to catch her breath, did Justina realise that she was there.

Victoria looked at the painting.

"That's beautiful," she said when she could speak. "I wish I could paint like you. But I wouldn't wear such a paint-spattered smock. Really, you should throw it away."

Victoria plumped herself down on the ground next to the stool.

"Look, a letter from Peter!" She waved it at her sister.

Justina dropped her paint brush.

"Really? What does he say?"

3

She loved Peter's letters. There were always descriptions of some aspect of his life that sounded so different from the mundane world of Surrey.

"He wants me to go and visit him."

Victoria handed over the sheets of paper and Justina scanned them eagerly.

"Fancy his Commanding Officer's wife inviting you to stay with them," Justina exclaimed. "Did you note his comment that you will get on very well with Mary, their daughter? Hasn't he written about her before? Do you think he wishes to make an offer for her?"

Victoria shrugged.

"How can one tell?" She arranged the folds of her muslin skirt neatly around her legs.

"When are you going?"

"Oh, Justina, I don't want to go."

"*Not want to visit India*?" Justina could hardly believe her ears. "But think of everything we have heard about from Peter – the elephants, the strange flowers and trees, the mountains and rivers, the incredible palaces, the glorious landscape. And the spices!"

"Think of the insects, the snakes, the heat!"

Justina looked down at the letter she held.

"Peter says it will be very exciting, lots of parties and junketings."

She smiled at her sister.

"I cannot possibly leave England now," Victoria said with a catch in her breath. She glanced demurely up at her sister through her eyelashes. "You do understand?"

"No," Justina replied bluntly.

She had a very deep voice. Her father loved it and said it was very soothing to listen to, but one or two of the young men she had been met had seemed a little taken aback when

THE LATE DAME BARBARA CARTLAND

Barbara Cartland who sadly died in May 2000 at the age of nearly 99 was the world's most famous romantic novelist who wrote 723 books in her lifetime with worldwide sales of over 1 billion copies and her books were translated into 36 different languages.

As well as romantic novels, she wrote historical biographies, 6 autobiographies, theatrical plays, books of advice on life, love, vitamins and cookery. She also found time to be a political speaker and television and radio personality.

She wrote her first book at the age of 21 and this was called *Jigsaw*. It became an immediate bestseller and sold 100,000 copies in hardback and was translated into 6 different languages. She wrote continuously throughout her life, writing bestsellers for an astonishing 76 years. Her books have always been immensely popular in the United States, where in 1976 her current books were at numbers 1 & 2 in the B. Dalton bestsellers list, a feat never achieved before or since by any author.

Barbara Cartland became a legend in her own lifetime and will be best remembered for her wonderful romantic novels, so loved by her millions of readers throughout the world.

Her books will always be treasured for their moral message, her pure and innocent heroines, her good looking and dashing heroes and above all her belief that the power of love is more important than anything else in everyone's life.

"Love is timeless from the moment of creation to beyond the end of infinity."

Barbara Cartland

they first heard her.

"Teddy!" exclaimed Victoria.

"You mean, he's going to propose?" Justina asked, her voice rising in excitement.

Edward Bathurst was a dashing young officer Victoria had met during her Season. Nearly two years older than Justina, she had come out a year before her.

Victoria was very pretty and she had a number of young men paying her attention, but Edward was the most persistent.

Victoria flushed, looked down at her skirt and made a few pleats in the material.

"He, well, he said he was going to approach Papa."

Justina gazed at her sister, her expression doubtful.

"Vicky, are you certain Teddy is what you want?"

Edward was very pleasant, but Justina did not find him at all exciting.

"What do you mean?" Victoria bridled. "He is – he is the most fantastic man."

"That's what Elizabeth thought about Philip."

"Justina! How *can* you compare Teddy with Philip?"

Justina picked up her sketch book and looked at the half-finished painting.

"Vicky, is love really as wonderful as they say?"

"Oh," Victoria sighed and lay back amongst the bluebells. "I cannot tell you how thrilling it is."

Justina looked at the blonde curls that tangled with the blue of the flowers. People said to her that she must envy her sister's hair. Her own was copper-coloured and curled far too strongly to be wound into ringlets.

"Tell me all about love," Justina demanded. "Did your heart beat faster the moment you met Edward?"

"Not at first. I thought he was very good-looking, but so were lots of the other men I met. But gradually he seemed to – well, I realised that it was him I wanted to call on me, him I wanted to talk to, him who, *yes*, made my heart beat faster."

Victoria turned over onto her stomach, picked a bluebell and started removing the little bells.

"You cannot describe love," she murmured dreamily. "You just know when it comes along."

"How do you know?"

"You can only think of the one person and when your eyes meet you get this funny, wonderful feeling in the bottom of your stomach." She blushed. "It is so exciting and also a little frightening."

"Frightening?"

"It is almost as if something in you is going to erupt."

"Like a volcano?"

Justina was astonished, it all sounded very strange to her.

"Something like that. And when you are with the one you love, everything seems perfect. It's as though the sun is always shining."

"And that's what it is like when you are with Teddy?"

"*Yes, yes, yes*!" Victoria cried.

She drew up her knees and hugged them, a dreamy expression on her face.

"And you think that your love is going to last for ever?" Justina's deep voice sounded very doubtful.

"Of course!"

"And do you think Elizabeth felt like that when she married Philip?"

"That is what she said."

"In that case, I don't think you can trust such feelings."

6

"It's not Elizabeth's fault, it's that Philip is *such* a swine."

"Vicky! Elizabeth surely didn't say that!"

"Of course not, it is something I overheard Papa say to Mama."

Elizabeth, the eldest Mansell daughter, had been married for five years. A most striking girl, she had been the *debutante* of her Season. Sir Philip Masson was tall, dark and very handsome.

Lord and Lady Mansell were delighted when Philip had proposed to Elizabeth. Their daughter was deeply in love with him and the elaborate wedding that took place seemed to promise a fairy-tale life for the happy couple.

Alas, by the end of the first year, Justina could see that her sister was far from happy.

The family saw nothing of her husband. He appeared to live most of the time in London and Justina realised that her sister was deeply miserable, but the situation was not one that was ever discussed.

"You are sure Teddy couldn't change the way Philip has?" Justina asked anxiously.

"He couldn't possibly," retorted Victoria indignantly.

"I don't see how you can be so confident. I don't think you can trust men and I am definitely not going to get married."

"When you fall in love, you will feel different."

"I cannot imagine falling in love. I shall be an old maid," Justina asserted cheerfully. "I'll come and look after your children and help Mama with her hospital and write letters for Papa."

"But you won't enjoy not being married and never having a life of your own. You know Mama is always worrying that you never seem to encourage any of the young

7

men we meet. She says it is so important that we all make suitable marriages and do not remain on her hands."

Justina said nothing.

"It is *you* who must go to India," announced Victoria. "That is what I came to tell you."

Justina stared at her, her heart beating fast. This was the most exciting suggestion she had ever heard.

"Do you really think so?" She took a deep breath, "I would so love to go."

"And you must."

"But he asked *you*."

"Only because he thought I was the senior unmarried daughter. If he knew I was about to be engaged, he wouldn't have suggested I went. You know how fond of you he is."

Victoria rose gracefully and held out a hand to Justina.

"Come, Mama will soon be home and we can tell her that you are off to India."

*

When Lady Mansell was told of the projected trip, her first thought was that it would be too expensive for them to afford. Lord Mansell had recently suffered financial setbacks that meant they had to make economies.

Justina was devastated.

"But it should not cost a lot of money," she pleaded. "I need not travel First Class and staying with friends means I don't have to spend too much."

Lady Mansell smiled.

"Your brother talks of lots of parties and outings. You will need a large wardrobe. I have heard that people dress up much more in India than here. There will be other expenses as well, such as a personal maid."

"You know I do not care much about clothes," Justina

protested, glancing down at the faded cotton dress underneath her painting smock.

Lady Mansell looked at her and fingered the large diamond brooch she always wore at her throat.

"My darling," she said. "If you really don't mind not travelling First Class and you don't need too many evening dresses, I am sure we can find some way to send you there."

Justina's face was transformed.

"Do you really mean that, Mama?"

She hugged Lady Mansell so hard that her mother protested she had no breath left. Then Justina whirled Victoria round and round, chanting,

"*I can't wait, I can't wait to go to India!*"

It was decided that Justina would travel out in the early autumn, arriving in the Subcontinent when the weather was cooler.

Lord Mansell was delighted to hear of the plan.

"And I hope you will fall in love with an eligible man who will return your affection," Lady Mansell added. Then she sighed. "We would not want to lose you and I would hate it if you stayed forever so very far away, but it would be such a relief to know you were settled."

Justina thought that falling in love was a dangerous business, but she would like to please her Mama, who seemed to think it was very important she found a husband.

Maybe, just maybe, there would be someone in India she could feel about the way Victoria felt about Edward.

Soon Lady Mansell had turned out her wardrobe and produced a number of dresses she felt could be altered to suit Justina.

*

The following weekend the Mansell family had an unexpected visitor.

Victoria was sitting in the window sewing yet another of her mother's refashioned evening dresses for Justina to take to India.

"Good Heavens," she said. "I think it is Aunt Theodora's carriage."

"Really?" said Lord Mansell and putting down his copy of *The Times*.

Justina dashed to the window, in time to see the Viscountess descend and advance up the front steps.

She felt her heart drop.

Stifling the urge to run away and hide, she stood with a straight back and swore to herself that she would not allow herself to be intimidated.

The Viscountess swept into the room. She was a commanding figure.

"My dear," greeted Lady Mansell, but there was nothing affectionate in her tone.

Lady Mansell offered her cheek to be kissed and then returned the gesture.

"George, good to see you," the Viscountess said to her brother.

"You're looking well, Theo," Lord Mansell said. "Come and sit down."

Lady Mansell attempted a little light conversation. She was never at ease with her sister-in-law.

"You have heard of Victoria's engagement?"

Another regal nod of the head.

"I met the young man when she came out. The family is excellent – and I gather his Army career is promising."

Victoria flushed with pleasure.

"George, what's this I hear about Justina not travelling First Class to India?"

Lord Mansell looked unhappy.

"The cost," he said in an embarrassed murmur.

"I will not have a niece of mine lumped with the proletariat," announced Lady Elder. "I am happy to present her myself with a First Class return ticket."

Justina tried to protest that she not want to be indebted to her aunt, but her parents were thanking the Viscountess and sounding so grateful there was little she could say.

"It is nothing," Lady Elder said graciously. "Also, she must be accompanied by a maid rather than wait to take one on in India. There is Dorcas Spencer who has recently joined my household. She is currently acting as a downstairs maid but has ambitions to become a personal attendant.

"I gather," her aunt continued, looking pointedly at the tangle of Justina's hair, "that maintaining a *soignée* appearance over the four weeks of the journey to India is difficult in the extreme."

She paused for a moment.

"I recommend you collect items that can be discarded after wear. They can be thrown from the porthole. Also I intend to discover a married woman travelling by the same ship who can act as a chaperone – you never know what ambitious *nouveaux-riches* travel First Class these days, Justina may well require protection."

Justina stared at her aunt. She was making the voyage to India sound both exciting and extraordinary. It was going to be very different from life in Surrey.

The Viscountess turned to her niece.

"Justina," she said commandingly. "I have come to talk to you."

She looked at Lady Mansell.

"Perhaps we may walk a little in the garden."

It was not a question.

The September day was sunny with all the warmth of summer even though the leaves on the trees had just begun to turn.

Justina walked beside her aunt down the long lawn.

"I want to ensure," said Lady Elder, sounding full of the authority that always made Justina feel like a member of the lower classes, "that you realise exactly what is your duty to your dear parents."

Justina swallowed hard.

"My duty? Aunt, you know I always try to do what Mama and Papa want."

Lady Elder sniffed.

"You did not try very hard during your Season."

"I did!" protested Justina. "But it was so difficult, I had nothing in common with any of the other girls and none of the young men were at all interested in me."

"As I told you more than once during your Season, you are far too forthright in your views. You need to temper your comments, seek to discover what your companion, whether a male or a female, is interested in. Do not expect them to draw you out, it is up to you to oil the wheels of conversation. I am sure your dear Mama has told you this time after time."

Lady Elder stopped walking, turned to her niece and sighed deeply.

"My dear girl, I am not the ogre you seem to think me. I truly want your happiness. But you must realise that, without a good marriage, you have no future. Thanks to his recent setbacks, your father is unable to provide you with a sufficient income to enjoy life as a spinster, a difficult business at the best of times."

Justina tried to say that it would make her content, but her aunt continued without pause,

"No, the only way for you to have any sort of

12

independence and pursue the interests your intelligence would enjoy is to find a husband of means. Your Mama and Papa realise this and will not be happy until you are married to a suitable husband. I am sure that, with a little thought, you will appreciate this to be the case."

"But what if my husband turned out as unsatisfactory as Elizabeth's?" she blurted out.

The Vicountess drew her breath in sharply.

"That is the most unfortunate matter. There is a certain – " she paused, seemingly seeking the right word, before adding, "let us call it instability in the Masson family. Had we known of it earlier, your father would not have permitted the match."

It made no sense to Justina. She left the subject of Elizabeth and concentrated on the main issue.

"You are saying, Aunt Theodora, that unless I get married, Mama and Papa will be very unhappy?"

"Exactly! I knew that you would realise your duty when it was properly explained to you."

"And you think I will find a suitable husband in India?"

"If you comport yourself properly and present the right background, yes, you will. There are very many more men than women in India. Often women who have failed to find a match in this country travel there for the express purpose of engaging the interest of a man. Even those lacking in looks, family or education can find someone to offer for them."

Lady Elder put her head on one side and looked assessingly at her niece.

"When properly turned out, you have an attraction all your own. If you mind your tongue and your manners, even without the sort of settlement your father was able to make when Elizabeth married, you will be looked on as a very worthwhile catch indeed."

Justina instantly hated the phrase.

Worthwhile catch indeed!

If she did have to get married and her aunt had shown her that the alternative was not attractive, then it would only be to someone who loved her for herself.

So far no young man had shown the least interest in her. The future looked dark.

The thought of travelling to India to find a husband removed much of the joy that had surrounded the prospect for Justina, but there was no use in telling her aunt.

The thought of disappointing her parents was dreadful. How could she both satisfy them and retain her independence?

"And remember that news will always come back to me of any poor behaviour on your part," the Viscountess admonished her sternly.

Then she smiled at Justina.

"Cheer up, life aboard ship can be entertaining in the extreme. You will meet so many new people and even you will find a few who are interesting."

Until that moment, Justina had not given the actual journey to India much thought.

Now Lady Elder had made her wonder if life aboard ship might not be as exciting as visiting India itself.

After all, the four weeks it took to sail to Bombay was quite a time to spend in the company of strangers. Her fellow passengers would not be naïve *debutantes* and crass young men – they would be people of experience.

"Now, let me give you some advice on comporting yourself," her aunt interrupted her thoughts in commanding mode. "To start with, I should tell you that on the first night out – "

But Justina did not want any more advice.

"Aunt Theodora, I am most grateful to you," she said swiftly. "I know what a disappointment I was to you in London and I will try very hard to be a success in India. And don't worry about the voyage, I have been told all about life on board ship by one of our neighbours."

The advice had been limited to the recommendation to take ginger with her as it was a well-known palliative in case of seasickness and Justina could not imagine she needed to know anything more.

For the rest of the day, Justina bubbled with excitement and forgave the Viscountess for interfering in her plans.

What an adventure the voyage was going to be!

CHAPTER TWO

Justina was amazed at the size of the ship that was to take her to India. As she and her family walked down the quay-side, it seemed to tower over them.

"My word," exclaimed Lord Mansell. "I remember the ship I sailed in when I first travelled to Bombay was a minnow compared to this one. It was a steamship, of course, but it carried sails as well."

"Let us go aboard quickly," suggested Lady Mansell. "I cannot wait to see what your accommodation is like."

"Fancy it being a maiden voyage," said Victoria. "Oh, Justina, I almost envy you."

"Do you want to change places?" grinned Justina. "Leave your beloved Edward behind for India?"

Victoria slipped her arm through Justina's.

"Never! I cannot wait for next summer – for our wedding."

Justina no longer worried about Victoria's future happiness. Nobody witnessing her sister with her fiancé could doubt that they were truly in love.

Could, Justina wondered, she achieve the same sort of relationship?

She shivered as her aunt's words came back to her.

Since her talk with the Viscountess, Justina's excitement at the prospect of exploring India had been spoilt.

How could she enjoy discovering temples, painting new flora and meeting strange people if she was supposed to be finding someone to marry?

Lady Elder had left Justina in no doubt that it was her duty to contract a suitable alliance. But she was determined not to marry someone without being as much in love with him as Victoria was with Edward.

At least she did not have to worry about anything for the next four weeks as she sailed on this splendid new ship to India.

Justina turned to the maid her aunt had lent her.

"Isn't this exciting, Dorcas?"

"Ooh, miss, it ain't half big!" exclaimed Dorcas, clutching the brim of her hat firmly in her gloved hand.

The maid was a plump girl with a round face. When Justina had first met her she thought Dorcas looked at her rather doubtfully, particularly at her springy mass of copper hair.

"I do my best with it," she had said cheerfully, pushing it back.

"I am sure Dorcas will cope very well," Lady Mansell put in gently.

"My mother was a lady's maid and she's taught me everything," Dorcas added with a note of pride. "I'm sure Miss Mansell will be a credit to me."

Justina thought she would like to be a credit to her family.

Once they reached the main deck, an Officer checked Justina's ticket and instructed a Steward to show them to her cabin.

It was much larger than Justina had expected.

"Well, how very comfortable," said Lady Mansell as the maid placed Justina's overnight bag on the berth.

The Steward who had showed them to the cabin reappeared.

"I'll take you down to your quarters, miss," he said to the maid. "Mrs. Grange, your Stewardess," he said to Justina, "will soon be here to make your acquaintance. Call on us for anything you need, we are here to make your voyage as enjoyable as possible."

Justina smiled at him.

"What is your name?"

"Chappell, miss."

"You must be very proud of this beautiful ship. I hope you aren't too anxious that all of us passengers will spoil the new paint."

"We all hope we arrive looking as good as now."

He was about to leave when Lady Mansell stopped him.

"My daughter is being chaperoned by a Mrs. Arbuthnot. Do you know where we can find her?"

"Not at the moment, my Lady, but as soon as I have shown Miss Dorcas her cabin, I'll find out."

He led the maid out of the cabin.

"Don't let's worry about Mrs. Arbuthnot," said Justina, bouncing on the bed. "I can find her after we have sailed."

"My darling," said Lady Mansell, caressing Justina's cheek. "I will not be happy to leave you until I have met the lady who will have you in her care." She looked at her husband. "What did Theodora tell you about her?"

"She is travelling with two daughters," replied Lord Mansell, ticking points off on his fingers. "They are twins and have finished their schooling. Mrs. Arbuthnot's husband is Colonel of his Regiment and she has spent the summer in England with the girls, preparing them to return to India."

He paused a moment then gave a shrug to his shoulders.

"That is the total amount of information at our disposal."

"Does Theodora know her well?"

"My dear, I wish you had quizzed my sister," Lord Mansell said ruefully.

"So do I! But there was so little time. All I ascertained was that Mrs. Arbuthnot has been most helpful with one of Theodora's committees."

At that moment there came a knock at the cabin door and a woman entered.

"Lord and Lady Mansell? I am so pleased to meet you. I understand from dear Lady Elder that I am to take your daughter under my wing with my own precious girls."

"Mrs. Arbuthnot?" queried Lady Mansell.

"Oh, how silly of me, I should have introduced myself. Yes, I am indeed Leticia Arbuthnot. And this is Faith and Charity. Come and say hallo, girls."

She was a small woman with soft features but unexpectedly sharp eyes. Her travelling costume was neat without being particularly stylish and was topped by a handsome Paisley shawl, now slipping down her arms.

As Lord and Lady Mansell led the way out of the cabin, Mrs. Arbuthnot fluttered over to Justina and Victoria.

"Now, which of you delightful girls is my charge?" she enquired archly.

"I am Justina."

The sharp eyes inspected her.

"So like your dear aunt. I know you will get on famously with my girls."

Mrs. Arbuthnot looked round, but her daughters had followed the Mansells.

She gathered her shawl more closely around her shoulders and hurried after the others, continuing to talk over her shoulder.

"There will be plenty of time, my dear, for many a cosy chat. The voyage to India is so delightful for getting to know one's fellow passengers. You have, I hope, brought a deck chair? But of course, I need not have asked. Dear Lady Elder would see to that for you. So necessary to enjoy the restorative powers of sea air."

By this time the little party had made its way up to the main deck.

Justina clutched at Victoria's hand.

She was not at all sure that she was going to enjoy spending so much time with the chaperone her aunt had chosen for her. She seemed the type of woman who spent most of the time talking and already Justina could feel her head beginning to spin.

"Mrs. Arbuthnot," began Lady Mansell as the group gathered beside the railings. "I should so like to meet your daughters properly."

Though twins, Faith and Charity were not identical. They were a little taller than their mother and both pretty. Faith was the more attractive with smooth blonde hair and cornflower blue eyes. Charity's hair was not as golden as her sister's and her eyes were so pale they were almost grey.

"I hope we shall be friends," Justina said firmly.

"Delighted, I am sure," Faith and Charity chorused in unison with simpering smiles.

"We are so happy to welcome Justina into our little family for the voyage," Mrs. Arbuthnot was saying to Lord and Lady Mansell.

A crewman passed them blowing a whistle and called,

"All ashore as is going ashore. All ashore as is going ashore."

Justina became aware that the boat was throbbing. The engines had started. She turned pale. How was she going to be able to part from her family?

"We shall leave you to say your goodbyes," proposed Mrs. Arbuthnot. Instantly Justina forgave her for talking too much.

"Come, girls, we must see that Muffin has been properly kennelled. My little dog," she said to the Mansells. "You would not believe what a fuss there has been over bringing her on this ship. We must find someone to tell us where they have taken her."

Justina clung to her mother until the last moment.

"Remember, my darling, we would so love you to find someone you would like to marry, someone as suitable as Edward," she murmured, kissing Justina.

Justina swallowed a sigh and standing by the railings of the ship, she watched her family hurry down the gangway, the last to leave the ship.

Justina waved and waved until she could no longer see her family. Even when they were out of sight, she remained by the railings, looking back to where they had been standing.

Gradually the calm of the harbour waters gave way to a gentle swell. There was a strong wind blowing, but ahead of the ship the cloudy skies parted and sun streamed through.

Justina decided to return to her cabin.

There Dorcas, looking much paler than when they first came on board, was unpacking the case marked 'cabin' that had been delivered before they arrived.

As Justina entered, the maid took out an old woollen skirt and held it up in a disapproving way. Flinging it on the bed, she then removed a cambric shirt and a well-worn jacket.

"Why, miss," she said as Justina came in. "These must

have got in by mistake."

Justina flushed guiltily and braced herself against the door as the ship started to move gently up and down.

"No, Dorcas. I put those in. I know they aren't smart, but I find them very comfortable and I thought it might be important to have some clothes it didn't matter if the sea made wet."

"Well, miss, it isn't my place to say as they aren't right – *but they aren't*," Dorcas commented firmly.

She swallowed hard, hesitated and speaking more quickly, added,

"They don't suit your position, not as Lady Elder explained it to me." She stuffed them back into the case. "If her Ladyship has told me once exactly what you should wear at every stage of the voyage, she's told me a hundred times. That Steward, Mr. Chappell, he explained to me where the baggage 'wanted on voyage' is kept. They're opening it this afternoon and I'll go down and see what I can find – "

She stopped and put a hand to her mouth. The maid's pallor had now acquired a greenish tinge.

"Are you all right?" Justina asked anxiously.

"Sorry, miss," Dorcas gasped. Then, hand clamped to her mouth, she dashed out of the cabin.

Justina wondered if she should go after her, but thought that if it had been her, the last thing she would want was for someone to see her being seasick.

She looked out of the porthole.

You could hardly call the sea rough, nor the movement of the boat more than gentle see-sawing. But perhaps some people were more susceptible to its motion than others.

Justina wanted to see around the boat, but thought if she did so she might run into the Arbuthnots. There would be time enough to spend with them before they reached

Bombay.

Suddenly there was a bell ringing in the corridor and passengers were being called to a lifeboat station drill.

Justina found herself gathered together with no one she knew. The Arbuthnots had obviously been allocated to a different lifeboat.

Outside, someone clanged a gong to announce that luncheon was served.

Justina realised that she was hungry. She picked up her hairbrush and tried to straighten out the tangle the sea breeze had made of her hair. As she reduced it to some sort of order, the Arbuthnots knocked on her door.

"We thought we had better collect you," said Mrs. Arbuthnot. "Dear Lady Elder said you knew very little of how life is ordered on board ship and we were to be sure to look after you."

The Arbuthnots had removed their hats and outer garments. All three were wearing prettily pin-tucked shirts and Mrs. Arbuthnot had a cameo brooch pinned to her high-necked collar. Faith and Charity had both arranged their hair so that it fell in graceful waves from little combs high up on their heads.

Beside them, Justina felt a mess. Dorcas was going to have to work hard on her appearance for dinner that night.

"Now, dear," Mrs. Arbuthnot was saying as she led the way along the narrow corridor, putting out a hand to steady herself as the ship moved up and down.

"I have spoken to one of the Dining Saloon Stewards. When I explained that Lord Mansell's daughter was one of our party, he was very happy to arrange for us to have one of the small tables. So much more *recherché* than having to mix with anyone and everyone at the long table in the centre of the Saloon. We shall be so comfortable and can really get to know one another."

She smiled at Justina.

"I am sure you will approve. Such a little, one might almost say, machination. Don't you agree, girls?"

"Mama, you always know how these things should be organised," said Faith with a little sigh.

"You know how we hate having to talk to just *anyone*," added Charity.

Justina, not knowing what to say, gave an uncertain smile.

When they reached the light and airy Saloon, she understood what Mrs. Arbuthnot had meant. Down the centre ran a long table, already almost full with a variety of passengers. At the top of the Saloon was a large, oval table with only a few passengers seated round it.

"The Captain's table," Faith breathed in her ear.

Around that end of the Saloon were a number of small tables.

"This is how we should dine," gushed Mrs. Arbuthnot with a smile of satisfaction as they were shown to one set for four.

An astonishingly comprehensive menu was produced, but Mrs. Arbuthnot waved away the wine list.

"I don't think so, thank you. I am sure Lord Mansell would not approve of alcoholic refreshment for his daughter, would he, Justina? I may call you that, may I not?"

But before Justina could say anything, Mrs. Arbuthnot continued,

"Now, girls, can we see anyone we know among the passengers?" Then she gave a little smirk, "or anyone we want to know?"

Faith leaned gracefully towards Justina.

"Mama is certain Charity and I will meet our fate before we dock at Bombay," she whispered, her voice fading away at the end of her sentence.

"Your fate?"

"A suitable husband," Charity joined in, sounding excited.

"Amongst the passengers?"

It had not occurred to Justina that the voyage to India might introduce her to an eligible young man.

Could this beautiful boat with its splendid decorations and spacious luxury provide the background to romance?

She pushed the thought away.

She did not want to have to think about suitable husbands until she reached India. But it sounded as though the Arbuthnot girls did.

"Are there any young men who are – " Justina hesitated, wondering how to phrase it. "Young men you could fall in love with?"

Faith gave a tinkling laugh.

"Fall in love with? Mama, isn't Miss Mansell the sweetest thing?"

Charity stared at her.

"What a curious voice you have. I should not like to have such a deep one."

Justina flushed, but tried not to mind.

"You speak as though I had some choice in the matter," she retorted.

Faith said in a soft voice,

"So far I have not had much opportunity to find out details of our fellow passengers. But part of the fun of the voyage is finding out who is who."

Mrs. Arbuthnot suddenly gave a start.

"Why," she said, "surely that is Sir Thomas Watson?"

Justina looked round.

Coming into the Saloon and heading in their direction was a tall man of striking appearance. Fair hair was slicked back from a broad brow. He had the face of a Grecian statue and his eyes were a sparkling dark brown.

Mrs. Arbuthnot gave a small wave.

"Sir Thomas," she called in a clear voice that carried above the clatter and chatter.

He looked around, hesitated and then approached the Arbuthnot table.

"Dear lady, what a pleasant surprise," he said and bowed over her hand.

"Dear Sir Thomas, I thought you had long since returned from London to Bombay. In the Colonel's last letter he wrote that he hoped to meet you when he next had the opportunity of travelling down there."

"Still stationed on the Afghan border?"

"Alas, yes. I don't think you have met our daughters, Faith and Charity? They have just finished school in England."

"What an unexpected pleasure," Sir Thomas said and there was something in his tone, a subtle suggestiveness, that made Faith and Charity simper in a way Justina already found infuriating.

Sir Thomas bent over each of their hands in a manner she thought of as Continental.

He straightened up and looked directly at Justina with a question in his eyes.

"Is this another daughter?" he asked with a laugh.

"Why I have just said that already she is almost one to me. This is Lord Mansell's daughter, Justina, who is travelling to visit her brother in India. Her aunt, the dear Lady Elder, requested me specially to look after her."

"Lord Mansell? I am delighted to meet his daughter."

This time it was Justina's hand he raised almost to his lips.

She felt his breath warm the back of her hand and a very strange feeling flooded through her. It was the sort of excitement she felt when her horse went for a high fence.

"Do you know my father?" Justina's voice deepened even further as it always did whenever she was struck with strong emotion.

"We belong to the same Club," he answered and his eyes seemed to laugh at her, as if he found her voice amusing. "Are you going to India for the first time?"

"My brother is a Subaltern, serving in the Central Provinces. I am going to visit him."

"What an exciting prospect for the Central Provinces as well as for you."

At the look in his eyes, Justina flushed. She was not used to admiration from men.

"Are you looking forward to discovering India?"

All the bustle of the Saloon faded away. Justina found she wanted to talk to this attractive man. She felt he would have interesting stories to tell her.

"Yes – " she started to say, but Mrs. Arbuthnot interrupted.

"Sir Thomas. Will you not join us for dinner tonight? We should all love to hear of your plans for when you reach Bombay."

He gave a glance around the table that seemed to include all three girls.

"Why, nothing would give me greater pleasure. Here was I thinking that, though this brand new ship is most beautiful, there was no one amongst the passengers to interest me. Four weeks of boredom, I thought. Then, lo and behold, in an instant, everything has changed. Now I can look forward to a most pleasurable time with three, no, four, most attractive females."

Mrs. Arbuthnot flushed with pleasure.

"Until tonight, Sir Thomas."

He gave a bow and continued to his table.

"Well, girls," Mrs. Arbuthnot sighed with pleasure after he had left. "Now we know we are in for a most entertaining voyage. How kind of him to say that you, too, are attractive, Justina."

"Oh, Mama, you are not being fair," piped up Faith. "Justina's hair is a little wild, but her freckles couldn't really be called disfiguring. It's a pity her eyes aren't blue, but they are quite large."

"Please do not talk about me as though I was not here," Justina countered stiffly. Inside she was boiling with anger.

"Oh, what does it matter what Justina looks like," said Charity. "Tell us about Sir Thomas, Mama."

"Sir Thomas Watson, Baronet, my dears." Mrs. Arbuthnot spoke in a breathy whisper. "Impeccable background, he can trace his family back to William the Conqueror, I believe, and a most successful business man."

She paused for a moment.

"Doing what, Mama?" asked Faith expectantly.

Justina was just as interested in Sir Thomas as the twins.

He had made her feel attractive as no other man had ever done.

"Oh, whatever his business is," Mrs. Arbuthnot said vaguely. "Import – export, you know. His house in Bombay is one of the largest and his carriage is simply splendid."

"Is he married, Mama?" queried Faith.

"*Why, no*! He is the most eligible bachelor in Bombay, if not the whole of India. And he is to dine with us tonight!"

Faith and Charity looked just as excited as Justina felt.

For once in her life she had met a man she actually looked forward to talking to. She was sure he could tell her all about India.

She seldom met men who had seen her father in action.

Could he have been in the House of Lords' Gallery at the same time as herself and her mother? Justina had been there several times.

It was always a pleasure to hear her father speak. Lord Mansell knew how to command the attention of his audience and put over clear and concise arguments.

But Justina was sure if Sir Thomas had been in the Gallery at the same time, she would have noticed him.

As soon as dessert was over, Mrs. Arbuthnot rose.

"My dears, what a thing, we shall have to try and make the most of ourselves this evening, we owe it to Sir Thomas. We must rest this afternoon."

Justina went to see if her maid had brought order to her cabin. If she had not already managed to unpack some of her evening dresses, she must do so immediately.

Dorcas was not in the cabin.

A Steward gave Justina instructions for finding the Second Class accommodation.

The maid was sharing a cabin with several other women. She, though, was the only one present. She lay on her berth, eyes closed, her face a pasty white.

Worried, Justina asked if there was anything she could do to help. In a voice so faint it could only just be heard, Dorcas said that she wanted to die and please to leave her alone.

Justina found the Stewardess for her cabin.

"Oh, miss, she's a one. Ship's hardly moving at all and she's like death warmed up and not so warm at that. Nothing

29

to be done, I'm afraid, until she adapts to the motion. I'll look after her, don't you worry, but it'll probably be days before she's any great shakes. We're in for a bit of a blow, is my understanding."

Justina resolved to make every effort not to disgrace her family that evening.

She might not be as attractive as the Arbuthnot girls, but her grey satin dress, once part of her mother's trousseau, had been refashioned with great style. What a pity, though, that Dorcas would not be available to do anything with her hair.

*

In his First Class cabin, Lord Castleton pushed away the pile of official papers he had been studying and stretched out his arms.

Ever since the ship had sailed that morning, he had been working. Lunch had been a sandwich and a glass of beer at his desk.

Now he was tired.

He looked at his watch and wondered whether to order supper to be served in his cabin.

Even as he considered this question, he seemed to hear a little voice at the back of his mind saying, 'go to the Saloon, Marcus, it will do you good.'

It was what Ariadne, his wife, would have said had she been here.

Lord Castleton had been widowed for five years now. Ariadne had died giving birth to their still-born son.

He had been devastated.

They had been so close, quite often each could anticipate what the other would say. Now he had adjusted to his loss, but he still knew that Ariadne would have told him he had been stuck in the cabin for long enough.

He quickly spruced himself up.

In the Saloon he was greeted by the Head Steward.

"Good evening, my Lord, I have arranged a table at the back for you."

"As always, Merton, you know my tastes."

"Of course, my Lord."

Passengers had only just started arriving for the evening meal.

Lord Castleton thought there was a good chance he could eat and leave before the noise grew too loud.

Settled at his table, he ordered one dish and a bottle of wine, then brought out some of the papers he needed to study before arriving in India.

Concentrating hard, Lord Castleton was quite unaware of the Saloon gradually filling up with passengers.

Until he heard the sort of buzz that signalled an unexpected happening, he looked up.

Coming through the room was a girl of seventeen or eighteen years. The first point that caught Lord Castleton's attention was the shock of copper coloured curls that surrounded her head in an aureole.

The second point was that no one seemed to have told the girl that passengers did not dress for dinner the first night at sea for she was arrayed in the most formal of evening dresses in grey satin.

It was immaculately cut, showed creamy white shoulders and displayed her willowy figure to perfection, but nothing could alter the fact that she had committed a *faux pas* of the worst sort.

As he heard murmurs of ridicule and the odd derisive laugh circulate the Saloon, Lord Castleton knew that Ariadne would have expressed more compassion for a girl hardly out of school.

Despite that wild head of glorious hair, this was definitely someone in need of protection.

As Lord Castleton watched, he saw the girl gradually realise that she was the only passenger who had changed into what his father would have called 'the full rig'.

Her huge eyes widened and shock flooded her mobile face as she recognised the magnitude of her error. She hesitated at a table for five near to Lord Castleton's, where sat a middle-aged woman with two girls of her own age.

Horror-stricken, the girl turned, as though to leave the Saloon. But the woman caught her arm, pulling her down to sit at the table.

"Don't make more of a fool of yourself than you already have," she snapped and her voice was cruel.

Lord Castleton found it difficult to credit her behaviour. The girl must be travelling with her, so why had she not explained what was expected?

He beckoned to the Head Steward.

"My Lord?"

"Who is the young lady who came in just now in evening dress?"

"Miss Justina Mansell, she is the daughter of Lord Mansell, my Lord."

"Thank you, Merton."

Lord Castleton knew Lord Mansell.

About two months ago they had shared a whisky at the House of Lords and talked about the very aspect of India that had brought him on this voyage. At the time he had not known he would be sent on this diplomatic mission, but he remembered Lord Mansell mentioning that a daughter of his was travelling out to spend time with his soldier son.

Could not the man have organised a better chaperone for his daughter?

Lord Castleton gathered his papers together and rose, waving away the Steward that hurried up to his table.

The girl was sitting with downcast eyes. He could imagine her embarrassment. No doubt she was hardly able to speak.

So far food had not been served to her table, it seemed they were waiting for the fifth member of their party.

"Miss Mansell, isn't it?" Lord Castleton began. "I am a friend of your father's and I am delighted to make your acquaintance."

Justina looked up and he was taken aback at the expression in the grey eyes that dominated her face. Far from being embarrassed, they blazed with anger.

"Will you allow me to introduce myself," he continued smoothly. "Marcus Castleton." He gave a slight bow. "And may I compliment you on the speed with which your maid has unpacked? There are few passengers on the first night at sea who are able to appear so beautifully turned out."

The first hint of a smile.

"You are too kind, sir. If my maid had not been completely overcome with seasickness, she would no doubt have explained that most passengers take the easy path and spared me the effort of dressing. But I am delighted to meet a friend of my father's. Please, may I introduce my fellow travellers?"

Mrs. Arbuthnot was all of a flutter.

"So delighted to meet you, Lord Castleton. The Colonel and I were at a Vice-Regal reception with you a few years ago in Bombay.

"But so charming to know we are all to be sailing together for the next four weeks. You must join us for dinner one night, I shall insist, my Lord."

Too old a hand to be caught making promises he had no intention of keeping, Lord Castleton murmured something about the pressures of work that had followed him on board and took his leave.

As he turned away from the table, he gave Justina a smile and found that she was grinning at him in a way that suggested she knew exactly what he thought of Mrs. Arbuthnot.

She was a girl with grit and he thought how much Ariadne would have liked her.

Delighted not to be leaving her in tears and conscious his status had gone some way towards rescuing her reputation, he threaded his way through the Saloon.

"Castleton!"

Lord Castleton stopped.

"Sir Thomas Watson," he said coldly.

"Travelling on the same ship, by Jove! What a coincidence."

The man seemed no more pleased with the encounter than he was.

"You look as though you have finished your meal, but no doubt we shall meet again. A ship is a small place."

It was a sentiment with which Lord Castleton could heartily concur. Even this ship, larger than any he had so far travelled on, was far too small to avoid those he would rather not encounter

As he made a curt acknowledgement and continued on his way, he wondered how much longer the man would be travelling First Class. The story going around was that Sir Thomas had made a series of unfortunate business moves and was on the point of bankruptcy.

Lord Castleton had not been surprised to hear this news as the man could not be trusted, either with business or with women. No doubt he would now be on the lookout for a rich wife to see him through his troubles.

Just before he left the Saloon, Lord Castleton could not resist turning back to look at the remarkable girl who had graced the room in her finery.

He felt more than a moment's unease as he saw that Thomas Watson was now seated at her table.

*

Justina watched Lord Castleton leave the Saloon with regret.

She would never forget her sense of humiliation as she realised that, instead of bringing credit on her family with her efforts to make the most of herself this evening, she had disgraced them.

She heard the derision, saw the contempt in the eyes of the other passengers and instinctively knew that Mrs. Arbuthnot's cruelty was a reaction to the embarrassment that Justina had caused.

After all, her chaperone should have warned her about the dress code.

But when Lord Castleton stopped at their table and spoke to her with such warmth, Justina had sensed that the mood of the Saloon had changed.

He must be a gentleman above reputation to achieve such a startling turn-around.

She might be regarded as an innocent but she knew that he had seen her predicament and had rescued her from public ridicule.

Moreover, he had looked at her with admiration in his eyes. After that, she had not cared what the other passengers thought.

But why had Mrs. Arbuthnot not made sure she was aware that no passengers dressed for dinner the first night out? She sat straight in her chair. Let other passengers think what they liked, Lord Castleton had admired her.

What a pity he had left so quickly.

As tall as Sir Thomas but with dark hair, he somehow managed to look more distinguished. His face was finely sculpted, he held himself with an unassuming authority and Justina could not forget the warmth in his eyes or how very deep blue they were.

She wondered if Mrs. Arbuthnot's silliness had driven him away or did he really have so much work to do? Would he spend the entire voyage working in his cabin as he had intimated?

She hoped very much that they would meet again.

Then Sir Thomas Watson arrived.

He bowed and wished them all good evening, but as his eyes took in Justina's appearance, a startled expression came over his face.

However it seemed that it was not her *faux pas* that had surprised him. He looked at Justina with admiration.

First Lord Castleton and now Sir Thomas. There must be something about her looks that appealed to older, more sophisticated gentlemen rather than the younger ones she had encountered during her Season.

"You are the most beautiful woman in the room," Sir Thomas whispered to her and his eyes seemed to bore into her in a way that made her feel unsteady.

"Oh, Justina has put us all into the shade," Mrs. Arbuthnot cooed sweetly but with a hint of steel. "But, then, what else should we expect from a member of the Mansell family? Such position, such wealth, such everything that is so desirable!"

Justina wanted to say that it was her aunt who possessed the riches. Once she would not have hesitated to do so but, now, having already committed such an error of etiquette, she did not like to contradict Mrs. Arbuthnot.

There was also another reason that stopped her.

This was a sudden thought that Lady Elder might have exaggerated her brother's financial state to enhance Justina's standing in Mrs. Arbuthnot's eyes. It did not seem all that likely, but Justina could not quite dismiss the possibility.

By this time Sir Thomas had sat himself in the empty place between Faith and Charity, which meant he was opposite Justina.

"Are you looking forward to returning to India?" he asked Faith.

She blushed and muttered something about being sad not to live in Bombay.

Justina was immediately interested and abandoned any thought of correcting the impression Mrs. Arbuthnot had given of her father's wealth.

"Is Bombay very special?" she asked.

"Ah, Bombay," Sir Thomas said and his dark eyes sparkled. "You know the island was a gift to Charles II from his Portuguese wife? Would that every wife brought such a dowry!"

He laughed and for a moment there was a coarseness about him that took Justina aback.

Then an abrupt lurch of the ship had everyone grabbing at plates and cutlery to prevent them spinning to the floor.

More lurches followed.

Their meal arrived, but soon all three Arbuthnots laid down their knives and forks.

"You must excuse me," Mrs. Arbuthnot said rapidly as she rose. "I think I should say goodnight."

Faith and Charity also stood, looking pale and unhappy.

"Do you want to come, too, Justina?"

She felt no necessity to follow them.

"I feel fine," she said. "I am sorry you do not and I hope the sea will soon be calmer."

"Well," Sir Thomas said as he watched them hurry from the Saloon, followed by one or two other passengers. "I suppose I should say what a pity. Instead, I feel most fortunate to have you to myself. You really do not feel at all uneasy at the motion of the ship?"

"Not in the slightest," admitted Justina honestly, feeling flattered at being called beautiful. "Now, tell me more about Bombay."

She thoroughly enjoyed listening to him and asked eager questions about other aspects of India. She found herself laughing at much of what he said and was thrilled to realise she would see him frequently over the next few weeks.

When, however, Sir Thomas at the end of the meal suggested that they take coffee together in the ship's Lounge, she looked round the now nearly deserted room and decided it would not be wise.

She had made enough of a spectacle of herself already that evening.

"You won't?" he said in surprise. His eyes narrowed slightly. "I thought you were enjoying my company."

"Indeed, I was," Justina hastened to reassure him. "But it has been a long day."

She stood and picked up her beaded reticule.

"I am sorry you refuse my exceedingly well meant invitation," he said softly in a way that made Justina feel uncomfortable. "I am not a man who expects to be refused, especially when the lady is as beautiful as you are."

Justina took a step backwards.

"I – thank you – Sir Thomas," she stammered. "Perhaps we can have a cup of coffee together tomorrow instead?"

Immediately the slight sense of threat vanished.

"Of course, my dear. And of course you must be tired. I have to thank you for keeping me company this evening."

The ship gave another of its lurches and he put out an arm to help support her.

She shivered slightly at the touch of his sleeve against the bare skin of her shoulders.

"Be careful. Let me help you across the room."

She pulled away, half wanting the touch of his arm to remain, but nervous at where such familiarity might lead.

"Thank you, Sir Thomas, but I can manage quite well." Sir Thomas followed Justina out of the Saloon and accompanied her along the corridor towards her cabin.

Once there, she turned to thank him.

"No need for such a beauty to thank a poor Baronet for keeping her company," he said with a look that made her heart beat faster.

As Justina opened her cabin door, he remained standing close to her and for an instant she wondered if he expected to come inside.

She pushed away such a ridiculous thought, gave a dextrous flip of her gown's skirt and moved lithely into the cabin.

With a last goodnight, she closed the door.

Alone, she chided herself for fearing such a move from a gentleman like Sir Thomas.

The prospect of meeting him again sent her to bed with a delightful feeling of expectation.

CHAPTER THREE

When Justina woke the next morning, it was to find the ship pitching up and down in a most disconcerting manner. Several of her possessions, instead of staying where she had left them, were rolling around on the floor.

After a little, in fact, she realised that she found the pitching and tossing exhilarating and she did not feel in the least seasick.

She drew back the curtain from the porthole. Rain lashed at the thick glass. Through it could be seen dark grey tossing waves of foam-flecked water.

Then she remembered her humiliation of the night before.

Her face burned as the moment came back to her when she realised what a mistake she had made. If it had not been for Lord Castleton's intervention, she would have felt an outcast.

He had been so kind.

She had a delightful feeling in her breast as she thought of his tall, aristocratic figure and the kind way he had spoken to her. She would have to tell her father when she wrote to him that they had met.

Then there had been Sir Thomas. What an good-looking man! And he had made her feel so attractive.

He had told her she was beautiful!

It was the first time anyone had said that to her. He had been almost *too* attentive.

Suddenly the door to her cabin crashed open.

Justina clutched the bedclothes to her chest half expecting it to be Sir Thomas.

But instead it was her Stewardess, Mrs. Grange.

"Good morning, miss. How are you feeling?"

"I am fine, but I don't know about the ship."

"It's only the Bay of Biscay, miss," Mrs. Grange informed her, holding onto the door frame. "Known for tossing us around a little."

"A little?"

"We've sailed through much worse than this. Now, I can bring you rolls, some orange juice and a bottle of water – or beer – for breakfast, but if you want coffee, I'm afraid you'll have to go to the Saloon."

The thought of hot coffee was enticing and Justina said she would dress and have breakfast in the Saloon.

She put on the woollen skirt and jacket that Dorcas had so despised, thinking how sensible she had been to bring them.

Just as she was leaving her cabin, Mrs. Grange appeared again.

"Message from Mrs. Arbuthnot, miss. Presents her apologies. She and the Miss Arbuthnots are laid right low. Asks if your maid could exercise her little dog."

Justina brightened.

She dismissed the idea of Dorcas walking their dog as she would be in a worse state than the Arbuthnots, but it would be a delightful activity for herself. She sent a message back to tell Mrs. Arbuthnot not to worry about Muffin.

The Dining Saloon was almost empty.

The Steward asked Justina if she would like to sit at the long table. At the far end were two young men tucking into plates of bacon and eggs.

Much further down the table was an elderly man reading a newspaper over toast and coffee. He had long sideburns and a large bald patch.

She went to sit beside him and he smiled at her.

"I like to see a young gel with sea legs. Come for a *chota hazri*, have you?"

"*Chota hazri*?"

"A little breakfast. Or perhaps a large one?"

"I've just learned my first Indian words!"

"That's the way! Many of the Indian servants don't speak English and you will need to learn at least some simple phrases if you are to get on with them."

The elderly man introduced himself as Frank Wright.

"Travelling back to Bombay. I am afraid the wife is suffering from *mal de mer*, as it seems are most of the passengers."

"I am Justina Mansell. Do you know India well?"

"Lived most of my life there – in the Indian Civil Service."

She was delighted to meet someone else who could tell more her about India and she passed an enjoyable breakfast learning about the difficulties of organising the Indian Empire.

At the end of the meal she asked Mr. Wright how she could find where a dog would be kennelled for the voyage.

Instantly he clicked his fingers for the Steward and soon Justina received directions on how to reach the upper deck.

"Do you want me to come with you?" Mr. Wright asked her. "It's blowing a bit out there."

She smiled and said she would be fine on her own.

"I expect Mrs. Wright needs you to see how she's getting on and I have to check on my maid." Then added hastily, "and Mrs. Arbuthnot and her daughters, of course."

"Of course."

Justina went immediately to check on Dorcas. Her maid's cabin was now fully occupied with moaning and groaning women. Dorcas, though, seemed worse than them.

It was a relief to leave the airless and foetid cabin. Justina thought if she had stayed any longer in there, she would begin to feel seasick herself!

The Arbuthnots' cabin was not much better.

She told them not to worry about the dog and escaped as soon as she could.

She put on an outer coat and found her way to the upper deck where the kennels were kept. Once in the fresh air, she breathed deeply and tried to forget the poor souls who had succumbed to seasickness.

There were four kennels secured near one of the funnels, but only two were occupied. A terrific barking from a large dog greeted her as she arrived, but the little terrier was silent.

She lay with her nose between outstretched legs and looked miserable.

A Steward gave her a lead and opened the kennel. She reached in and picked up the dog. As Justina lifted her, she could feel her shivering badly, but it did not stop her licking her face in welcome.

"Come on now, let's go for a bit of a run."

Justina soothed the small animal and soon the shivering stopped. She attached the lead and, hanging onto the railings, took Muffin round the upper deck a couple of times. She trotted through the rain beside her happily enough.

But when she was taken back to the kennel, the shivering started again and she uttered little whimpers of distress.

Justina hated the idea of putting her back into the dark and chilly kennel. She looked around the deck. The Steward was nowhere in sight. Quickly, she shut the door and closed the padlock.

Then she slipped Muffin under her jacket and arranged it so that it hung loosely with no betraying bulge.

The rain seemed relentless and Justina was very happy to return to the warmth and safety of the ship's interior. She was also happy to see that her bed had been made up and the cabin looked beautifully tidy.

Locking the door, Justina rescued the dog from inside her jacket. There were more frantic lickings of her face.

She took a cushion from the little sofa and put it down in a corner.

"Your bed," she told the dog.

Muffin looked up at her, her head on one side and then arranged herself comfortably on it. Despite the motion of the ship, she seemed to fall asleep almost immediately.

Justina looked at her for a few moments and satisfied that she would be happy for a while, found her sketch book and some chalks.

The main lounge was almost empty. Only two elderly men were there, fast asleep in comfortable chairs.

Through the huge windows were marvellous views of the stormy waves with crests of white foam. In the distance, Justina could see a large sailing ship coming towards them.

Then she turned to a new page in her sketch book. Soon she was lost in capturing the wildness of the scene and the ship having a hard time making way against the wind with one small sail.

"Well, well," said a familiar voice a little later. "Still not suffering from *mal de mer* I see."

She looked up to find Sir Thomas standing beside her.

"Good morning," she greeted him.

Wearing a smart blazer and a cravat, he looked very dashing.

"Quite an artist, aren't you?" he said, taking a look at her sketch.

Justina forgot the slight unease she had felt in his company at the end of the previous evening and grinned. She had spent enough time on her own and was delighted to see him.

He sat down in the chair next to Justina and summoned the Steward.

"Now, you must join me in a brandy, nothing better for settling the stomach."

"But my stomach does not need settling – though I thank you," Justina responded hastily. "Are you feeling under the weather, Sir Thomas? Is that why you need brandy?"

"I am very good sailor," he protested. "I hope you don't think I look as though I am a victim of the ship's motion like most of our fellow passengers."

He looked around the almost empty lounge.

Justina told him the truth, which was that he looked very well.

"I haven't seen Mrs. Arbuthnot or her girls this morning."

"Victims," replied Justina succinctly. "I have been walking their dog."

"Good Heavens, don't tell me you like animals?"

"Don't you?" Justina was amazed as she could not imagine anyone not liking man's best friend.

"Horses are fine for getting me around, in fact, I rather pride myself on my equestrian abilities. For the rest," he gave a shrug, "I'd rather not come into contact."

Justina was about to start arguing with Sir Thomas when he continued,

"I prefer to spend my time with attractive members of the human race." He bared his teeth at her in a way that Justina hoped he meant for a joke. "*You*," he added, "are one of the most beautiful and unusual women it has been my privilege to meet for a long time."

Justina gazed at him in astonishment. Exciting as it had been to hear him call her beautiful last night, it was extraordinary to be told again in the morning! It almost persuaded her that he meant it.

He moved his chair closer to hers.

"Last night you looked wonderful. I was so glad the Arbuthnots had to leave the table as they might have been insulted by the way I only had time for you."

He smiled at her, a dangerous smile that made her heart flutter in a way it never had before.

"You have the most astonishing eyebrows. In another woman they might dominate her face too much, but yours are perfect, they balance the straightness of your nose and the size of those eyes, which have a depth of grey like the sea today."

Justina could not stop staring at him.

Never before had any man spoken to her in such a way. One part of her wished him to continue, another was afraid of where it might lead.

She gave a nervous laugh.

"Now you are talking nonsense, Sir Thomas. Especially when I am dressed in my oldest clothes, I only brought them in case of rough weather."

"When I look into those remarkable eyes, I cannot see

anything else," he mumbled.

Justina found herself almost unable to think. She swiftly gathered up her chalks and sketch pad.

"I – I must go – go and change before lunch is served. I cannot enter the Saloon dressed like this," she managed to say.

"No one will notice."

Sir Thomas tried to catch hold of her arm.

But Justina evaded his hand and, helped by the way the ship lurched, moved quickly out of the Lounge.

Gradually her heart stopped beating so rapidly and her breath came back.

She fought the motion of the ship as she made her way back to her cabin and wondered about her feelings.

Was this the sort of emotion Vicky had felt when she fell in love with Edward? Or Elizabeth when she was with Philip?

But at the thought of her eldest sister's disastrous relationship, Justina felt panic.

She would have to be careful next time she met Sir Thomas not to allow him to raise such exciting feelings in her again.

Approaching her cabin, Justina became aware of a commotion. Her door was partly open and several Stewards and Stewardesses were outside, exclaiming and offering advice.

From inside the cabin came a furious mixture of barking and growling.

Muffin!

"What is happening?" she demanded.

"Miss Mansell, there is a dog in your cabin and it is preventing access," Chappell said, fired up to the point where he was prepared to forget that she was one of his cherished passengers.

"I am so sorry," she muttered and slipped past him.

Muffin was just inside the door, feet firmly planted on the floor, ears on end, sharp teeth bared, determined to repel all who would attempt to enter.

Justina bent down and scooped her up.

"There, there," she cooed soothingly. "No need to be on guard, these are friends."

"Thank you, miss," Chappell said stiffly.

"I do apologise," Justina replied, stroking a panting Muffin. "She thought she was protecting my territory, you see."

"I don't knows about that, miss. What I do know is that animals ain't – isn't allowed in the cabins. That dog should be in a kennel on the top deck."

"But it's so cold and miserable up there, she was so unhappy." Justina started to get angry. "How can you condemn this poor little animal to such an awful fate when the weather is getting rougher and rougher?"

"Miss, it's the rules and if you won't obey them, I'll have to call an Officer."

"I don't care if you fetch the Captain, I am not taking Muffin back up there," Justina shouted.

Suddenly an authoritative voice broke into the argument.

"Will someone please explain what this noise is all about? I am finding it impossible to work in my cabin."

To Justina's amazement, Lord Castleton stood by the open door, a well-shaped eyebrow raised as he assessed the scene in front of him.

"Oh, my Lord, please help me," she blurted out impulsively, remembering how kind he had been the previous evening. "They are trying to insist that this poor little dog is sent back to those awful kennels."

Lord Castleton came into the cabin and looked at the terrier panting excitedly in Justina's arms.

"Is this your dog?"

"No, she is Mrs. Arbuthnot's."

"So what are you doing with her?"

"Mrs. Arbuthnot is seasick and sent me a message asking if Dorcas would exercise her."

"And who is Dorcas?"

"My maid, only she is seasick too, much worse than Mrs. Arbuthnot."

"So you took on the duty," he proclaimed as though the whole scene had now become clear to him. "And then decided that your cabin would be a more acceptable home for her than the official kennel?"

Justina looked up at him with relief.

"Yes, it was raining and cold and she was shivering and, well, I couldn't do anything else."

"You didn't like it up on deck so you decided that – what is this animal's name?"

"Muffin."

"So you decided that Muffin didn't like it either. Do you know what that process of deduction is called?"

Justina looked at him in surprise. What on earth was he talking about? Then suddenly she understood.

"Anthropomorphism?" she asked doubtfully.

"Good girl!"

"I don't know what you're on about, but that animal is not allowed in the cabins, my Lord," broke in Chappell.

"Leave this to me, will you, please?" he said firmly but politely.

"Right you are, my Lord, as long as you understand

49

ships' regulations."

"Quite," said Lord Castleton.

He waited until the little group had dispersed, but made no move to shut the cabin door.

"Thank you so much, my Lord," sighed Justina. She sank down on the little sofa. "I didn't know what to do."

He looked at her ruefully.

"What we have to do, I am afraid, is return this mutt to her kennel."

Justina could not believe her ears.

"She's not a mutt, surely you can see she is a Highland terrier. And surely you don't expect her to go back to that dreadful kennel?"

"I admit that the accommodation is not what that spoilt animal is used to, but I promise you she will settle down quickly. Her ancestors were used to far worse."

"But she isn't," Justina flared at him. "You are heartless if you condemn her to go back up there."

Lord Castleton sighed.

"Call me what you like, but I have a dog in the kennels myself and I am known as a lover of animals."

"I don't believe it!"

"You don't believe I'm a lover of animals?"

"I don't believe you have a dog up there. You couldn't have."

"Shall we go and see?"

Justina looked up at him. There was nothing threatening about the way he stood there, but somehow she found it difficult to refuse him.

"Yes, let's, then you will see exactly what I am talking about."

"I was up there earlier myself, giving Breck a walk,"

he said mildly, indicating the way into the corridor.

"Breck?"

"My dog. He is an Irish Wolf Hound. I expect to go hunting in India with one of the Maharajahs. I told him about Breck last time I was in India and he insisted I brought him on my next trip."

Justina was so interested in this story, she forgot to insist that he need not expect her to leave Muffin in the kennel.

As they climbed to the upper deck, she plied him with questions.

Lord Castleton seemed happy to tell her about hunting wild boar and the fabulous palaces he had stayed in.

It was still raining, but the rocking of the ship seemed to have quietened a little.

As they emerged, the Steward in charge of the kennels came up to them.

"Have you got the little dog, miss? I've been that worried, seeing that the kennel was locked with no animal in it."

"It's fine, Parsons," said Lord Castleton. "Miss Mansell has been good enough to introduce Muffin to me. Now I am going to introduce her to Breck. Would you be good enough to open both kennels?"

"Right away, my Lord. But I would ask you not to be too long as I'm not supposed to allow passengers on the deck in this weather."

"We will be very careful," responded Lord Castleton soothingly.

The Steward unlocked two of the kennels then stood by the funnel keeping an anxious eye on them.

"I am not leaving Muffin here," Justina said pointedly.

"Come and meet Breck."

He opened the door of his kennel and whistled. Out came a great, lanky and majestic looking brindle hound that bounded up to his master and gently licked his hand.

Lord Castleton took a firm grip of his collar.

"Shall we take them both inside for a few moments?" he suggested.

Justina was delighted. She was sure she could convince him that both animals should not be outside in this weather.

"Now, say hallo," he commanded his dog.

Breck looked up at Justina still holding Muffin in her arms and licked at her hand. He was so tall that it was an easy reach for him.

"Oh, you darling," she cried and caressed his head, feeling his coarse springy hair.

"Why don't you put Muffin down and let them meet."

Carefully she put Muffin on the ground. The little dog looked curiously at the huge animal and bared her teeth but did not growl.

Breck maintained a lordly disinterest for a few moments and then bent his head to sniff at the terrier. Muffin backed away and sat down while Breck circled her, sniffing gently and curiously.

As Justina watched, the two dogs seemed to reach an understanding. All at once Muffin started frisking around Breck and the huge hound settled to the ground so that their heads were on the same level.

Lord Castleton grinned at Justina.

"I think we can say they are now friends."

"Shall we take them both back to my cabin?" she asked hopefully.

He laughed.

"Come, Miss Mansell, you are too intelligent to expect

me to agree to that."

He looked at the two dogs, now lying head to head, the hound taking up most of the landing space.

"Let's get them put in adjacent kennels so they can be company for each other."

Justina looked up at him distractedly. She had meant to insist on taking Muffin back with her, whether he could smooth things over with the Stewards or not. But now she was not so sure.

Would little Muffin really be happy, though, in that draughty kennel?

"Are you sure they will be all right?"

His eyes as he looked at her were kind and she felt something inside her melt.

"Quite, quite sure."

Justina suddenly had an idea.

"Wait here. I'll be back in a minute."

It took her rather more time than a minute to return, but Lord Castleton was still on the landing with the dogs playing happily together.

He smiled as she came up the companionway.

"Got what you went for?"

"Yes!" She waved a wrap at him. "If we put this in Muffin's kennel, it will keep her warm."

"You have a very good heart. Giving up your wardrobe to a dog that isn't even your own."

"Pooh. I don't care about clothes nearly as much as animals."

"Looking at you last night, I would never have believed it!"

"Please, let us not mention that ever again, I felt humiliated."

She looked up at him shyly.

"And thank you for rescuing me."

"I did nothing. Everybody would have forgiven you for not knowing the form."

Lord Castleton was so grand and yet so approachable. She felt she could trust him in any situation.

It was a very different feeling from the one Sir Thomas inspired in her, much more comfortable and yet, in its own way, also unsettling.

Justina enveloped Muffin in the warm wrap and straightened up with the little dog in her arms. Lord Castleton looked at her with a humour and companionship that made her feel they were friends.

Lord Castleton spoke to the Steward and Muffin's kennel was moved so it was next to Breck's and the two dogs could see each other.

Justina organised the wrap inside and arranged Muffin in its folds. She took time to talk to her, saying that she was going to be all right, that Breck would keep an eye on her and that she would come back to see how she was.

The little dog looked up at her trustingly and did not seem at all distressed at having the door closed on her.

Justina stood up and apologised for taking so long.

"Not to worry. If we've made Muffin happier with her lot, it's time well spent." Then he pulled out his watch. "We can just catch lunch."

*

Lord Castleton led the way into the Saloon. He headed for his small table at the back of the large room, waving off Merton, who had hurried forward. Then he realised that Justina had stopped at the long table.

He was surprised to see her talking with another passenger, an elderly man with gold-rimmed glasses. He smiled as he saw the comfortable way she chatted to him.

"Shall we sit here?" he suggested.

Her large grey eyes looked pleased.

"May I introduce Mr. Wright, my Lord? He is a member of the Indian Civil Service."

"Delighted to meet you, Mr. Wright. I shall be having many meetings with the ICS during the next few months."

He sat down beside Justina, opposite the civil servant.

"How is your wife? Feeling any better?" asked Justina. "I think the motion of the ship has eased a little during the morning."

"Not enough," he replied ruefully. He polished off a piece of steamed pudding and rose. "I must go and see how she is, though I doubt I'll get more than a few whispered words of wishing for death from her. I trust you will enjoy your meal, it is a pleasure to see a young lady with such fine sea legs."

They watched him walk away.

Lord Castleton asked if Justina would like some wine and was amused to see her wrinkling her nose as she debated with herself over whether to accept his offer.

"It's very kind of you, my Lord, but I think my father would say alcohol should be restricted to the evenings. But, please," she added hastily, "do have some yourself."

"I will," he assured her and ordered a bottle of claret.

"I find I am very hungry," Justina confided in him. "But perhaps that is unladylike to confess."

"Does it worry you to be thought unladylike?" he enquired, amused at the unexpected nature of this girl.

"I am always being told how important it is to comport myself with due decorum," she said and looked at him through her long eyelashes, a proper picture of demureness.

"And you find that difficult?"

Justina sighed heavily.

"I want to say what I think, so many aspects of life are exciting and interesting, or make me angry. Instead of being able to discuss them with, well, with anyone, I am supposed to make commonplace comments."

Any of Lord Castleton's many friends would have been amazed to see him in conversation with a girl only just 'out'.

On the rare occasions he attended balls and dinner parties, he spent most of his time avoiding the attentions of husband-hunting mothers and *debutantes*.

The previous evening he had obeyed an impulse to rescue a girl who seemed, despite the style of her inappropriate gown, to be all at sea in every sense.

When he had been disturbed by the noise in the next door cabin, he had at first hardly recognised her. Gone was the elegant dress, exchanged for clothes more suited to a Second than a First Class passenger. Her flaming hair was drawn back in an unbecoming knot and her rigidly controlled demeanour had given way to unashamed passion – all on behalf of a small dog!

Once again he had obeyed an impulse. Instead of allowing the Stewards to send for a ship's Officer, who would have known exactly how to insist the dog was returned to its kennel and would probably have left the girl feeling bruised and resentful, he had taken charge himself.

What was it about her that caused him to behave in such a reckless fashion?

"Are you 'out'?" he asked her.

Justina gave another great sigh.

"My aunt, Lady Elder, gave me a Season last year. I am afraid I let her down badly."

"In what way did you let her down?" he asked

curiously. "I am sure your manners could not be found wanting and you have a remarkable presence."

She flushed, disconcerted at his remark.

"Presence, my Lord? My aunt would say I lacked tact and social graces." She lent towards him in her engagingly confiding manner. "Perhaps you know how to speak to girls who seem to have no thoughts in their heads beyond eligible men and the latest fashions, as I don't. And is it my fault if young men prefer blonde curls and simpering misses who never contradict a single thing they say?"

Lord Castleton laughed.

"No doubt you told them when they said something less than sensible?"

Justina grinned at him, perfectly at ease again.

"They would make the most asinine remarks, such as wasn't the weather perfect, or didn't I think the current Royal Academy exhibition such a topping lot of pictures? Most of the time I stood at the side of the dance floor watching other girls look at them as though they were Gods."

She gave a most unladylike snort.

Miss Mansell had a very mobile face and Lord Castleton enjoyed himself watching dismay gradually dawn over it.

"You see what a wretched grasp of etiquette I have," she said. "I should be asking you about yourself, why you are going to India, which I would dearly love to hear about, and thanking you again for sorting out poor Muffin instead of telling you how impossible I am."

"Are you impossible?"

"Mama and Papa are expecting me to attract a suitable husband on this visit to my brother. They are worried I shall end an old maid. I used to think that I would like to remain a spinster as that way I could think and say what I liked, but now I wonder if it might not be better to find someone I could love with all my heart. Then I would please Mama and Papa and be happy myself. Would that be impossible, do you think, my Lord?"

He was taken aback.

Not at the sentiments, he could understand those all too well, but that she should be expressing them to himself.

But this girl was simply talking to him as though he was her – damn it, as though he was her *uncle*! A man of her father's generation.

Lord Castleton was in his early thirties and nothing in his life so far had suggested young women could look on him as anything other than desirable husband material.

Until now!

He picked up his wine glass and drank deeply.

Justina was looking at him anxiously. She obviously expected a sincere response.

"Not at all impossible, Miss Mansell," he said quietly. "I was fortunate enough to enjoy a most loving relationship until death took my beloved Ariadne from me."

"What a tragedy," Justina sighed. She put a slim hand on his arm. "I feel so much for you."

He swallowed hard and cleared his throat.

"Thank you. And I hope that you will find someone you can love as deeply." He tried for a lighter tone. "I am sure you will meet a wide variety of single men during your time in India. Why not give them a chance to attract you. I am sure they will find you a delightful companion."

Then she proved that she had both tact and social skills by enquiring about the reasons for his visit to India.

He enjoyed telling her how he would be meeting many of the Maharajas.

The rest of the meal passed very quickly as he held her

entranced with tales of bejewelled and autocratic rulers.

"And you must try and see Jaipur," he suggested as their dessert plates were removed. "When the Prince of Wales visited there some twenty years ago, the town was painted a fetching shade of ochre and now it is known as the Pink City."

"How amazing! Fancy painting a whole town just because a foreign Prince was to pay a visit."

"Remember that he will be Emperor of India one day."

"I must say, though, that ochre doesn't sound very pink."

"It's the sun that gives it that special tinge."

"Oh, how wonderful it would be to see it at sunset," Justina clapped her hands, immediately entranced with the vision. "I must ask Peter if he can organise a visit."

Lord Castleton wanted to say that he would arrange it for her, but restrained himself.

"It is still raining and the motion of the ship is keeping most passengers in their cabins. Would you like to play some cards? Simple games," he added hastily. "I do not mean we should gamble."

Justina gave him one of her delightful grins.

"Vicky and I often play a sort of double-handed patience. I wonder if you know it?"

"You can show me and I am sure you can teach me quite quickly."

Justina could hardly believe that here she was playing cards with Lord Castleton. She in fact spent several hours with him in an atmosphere of great amiability. It was almost as though he was one of the family.

It was no doubt wrong of her to tell him all about her worries over finding a suitable husband, but he had not seemed to mind.

With a cry of triumph, Justina won the latest of their games. She glanced delightedly up at Lord Castleton and caught him looking at her with a warm smile.

All of a sudden, deep within her, she felt her heart stop and it was if the world halted in its motion.

Moments later her heart thumped back with a strange beat, the world continued its spinning and her breath returned.

But it was as if a layer of her skin had been removed, leaving her ultra-sensitive to the man sitting on the other side of the table. She was conscious of every breath he drew, every movement he made.

Justina gathered up the cards with trembling hands. She tried to shuffle them, but she had no control and they spilled everywhere.

Lord Castleton did not seem to notice anything strange. His attention was caught by someone who had just entered the Lounge.

"Well, well," said Sir Thomas. "I see you are having fun. Can I join your little party?"

Without waiting for an invitation, he brought a chair up to their table, sat down and started to help Justina gather together the cards.

His presence helped her regain some sort of control.

In one way she was pleased that Sir Thomas had arrived, but in another she resented him intruding on the happy time she had been enjoying with Lord Castleton.

"What is the game?" enquired Sir Thomas, shuffling the pack expertly.

Lord Castleton rose.

"I am afraid I have to return to my papers," he said and Justina could not understand why his voice was suddenly so cold.

"Have I said something?" Sir Thomas asked in a jovial voice.

"Not at all. It is unfortunate I have had to bring so much work with me. Miss Mansell, thank you for your company."

He gave Justina a small stiff bow and left the Lounge.

She felt abandoned.

Before Sir Thomas arrived, they had been friends, now it was as though he had been undertaking some kind of duty in being with her, a duty that the arrival of the other man had removed from him.

"I have to apologise for my clothes, Sir Thomas. As you can see, I have not been able to change."

He raised an eyebrow.

"You still look enchanting to me, but what prevented you?"

"There was some trouble with Mrs. Arbuthnot's dog. Lord Castleton helped sort things out. We were very late for lunch."

"Castleton helped you?"

"He was very kind."

Sir Thomas ran a thumb over the edge of the cards in a way that Justina found irritating.

She suddenly felt drained. It had been an exhausting day. Coping with the motion of the ship was tiring. The difficulties with Muffin had caused her a great deal of stress.

Then there was that heart-stopping moment with Lord Castleton that she could not understand, or why when he left so abruptly she should feel so lost.

And now there was Sir Thomas. She enjoyed the way he made her feel attractive, but he raised tensions in her that, again, she did not understand.

"I am so sorry," she said, rising. "I am afraid I must

have a rest. The ship rocks so much."

He looked up and she saw that he was angry.

"I understand, but you are not tired enough to play cards with Lord Castleton," he gave the title a derisive emphasis.

"But when I come along, suddenly you have to go and rest," he mimicked a mincing way of speaking that Justina did not feel resembled at all her straight-forward delivery. "Well, let me tell you that there is little to admire about Lord Castleton."

"What – what do you mean?"

Sir Thomas looked at her, his dark eyes serious.

"Perhaps I should not have spoken as I did, but I knew the late Lady Castleton very well – poor woman."

"Why do you say, 'poor woman' like that?"

"Because she was to be pitied, married to Castleton with his proud airs and political ambitions. She found life, shall we say, unsatisfactory."

Justina could not take in what he was saying.

"Ariadne was a beautiful woman, she could have had any number of men. She must have regretted her choice many a time, left on her own while Castleton danced attendance on his political masters, always at the House of Lords or in Whitehall instead of accompanying her to dinner or spending time at their country estate."

Sir Thomas gave a bark of a laugh.

"Don't let that smooth manner fool you, Castleton lacks a heart."

"I cannot believe – " she started to say when he interrupted her with a deprecating laugh.

"Of course you can't. You or the rest of the world." He sighed heavily. "Perhaps I see things differently because I was so fond of Ariadne."

He looked so sad that Justina in her impulsive way felt sorry for him. She could not, though, believe that Lord Castleton had been anything but a model husband.

"But I am keeping you from your rest." Sir Thomas rose. "I shall look forward to seeing you this evening. Perhaps if Mrs. Arbuthnot and her daughters are still not well, you will join me for dinner?"

Justina muttered something to the effect that he was very kind and left the Lounge.

The ship was now pitching and rolling more than ever and, even though she did not feel seasick, she was not sorry to lie on her bed.

On the other side of the bulkhead was Lord Castleton's cabin.

She wanted to go and ask him why he had left their card game so abruptly.

What had it had to do with the arrival of Sir Thomas?

Was he going to spend the rest of the voyage working in his cabin? She wanted so much to be able to talk to him again.

Sir Thomas had asked her to dine with him. The prospect was exciting but unnerving and, even more important, she was sure that her aunt would not approve.

When Sir Thomas looked at her with his dark eyes, she felt her heart begin to race, but he was a very unsettling companion.

Was he to be trusted?

CHAPTER FOUR

Before dressing for dinner that evening, Justina went to check on Mrs. Arbuthnot and her daughters.

All were still suffering from dreadful seasickness.

Blessing the fact that she seemed to be an excellent sailor, she returned to her cabin.

What was she to do now about this evening?

It must be wrong to accept Sir Thomas's invitation to dine with him, but she knew how persuasive he could be.

And what would Lord Castleton think if he saw her dining with Sir Thomas? Justina was not sure why she was so worried about this prospect but she was.

Agonising over her quandary, she fought her way along the pitching corridor back to her cabin.

Just before she reached her door, Lord Castleton came out of his cabin.

"Miss Mansell," he acknowledged her formally. "Finished your card game?"

"I haven't been playing," she replied hurriedly. "I had a rest and then went to see how Mrs. Arbuthnot and Faith and Charity were faring."

"Still suffering, I would imagine."

He sounded so kind and so much the friend she had spent such a large part of the afternoon with, Justina immediately forgot Sir Thomas's description of him as an unfeeling husband and felt emboldened.

"Lord Castleton, I have a problem," she began shyly.

"Not with Muffin, I hope?" he asked with a warm smile.

She shook her head.

"It's this evening."

Justina forgot about the heart-stopping moment she had felt earlier. She was certain now that this friend of her father's would be the best person to solve her dilemma.

"It's that Sir Thomas who has asked me to join him for dinner," she said shyly.

Lord Castleton's smile vanished and he stood very still.

"What have you said to Sir Thomas?"

"Only that it was kind of him, but I was not sure about this evening and – and then I left."

"I see."

Justina was about to say that he could not possibly understand the difficulty of her situation when the ship lurched particularly violently and she was pushed into Lord Castleton's arms.

He grasped her securely and she felt herself held close to his chest. Her head fitted neatly under his chin and she could feel his heart beating.

For a moment she imagined that his lips were kissing her hair.

"I am so sorry," she blurted out, amazed at the way her heart was beating.

"Now, what are we going to do about your problem?" he mused as though they had never been clasped in a close embrace.

Justina gazed at him hopefully.

"Do you want to dine with Sir Thomas?"

She shook her head vigorously.

"I enjoy his company, but I am sure my aunt, Lady Elder, would say it would be very unwise."

"I agree with her," he said composedly. "I also know that Sir Thomas is not a man who takes 'no' lightly."

"That is why I don't know what to do. If I have my meal in the cabin, he may well come down to see if I am suffering seasickness."

"I think I see a way to avoid any unpleasantness. When you are ready to go to the Saloon this evening, knock at my door and we will go through together."

It was a delightful idea, but she felt that Lady Elder would no more approve of her dining with Lord Castleton than she would her dining with Sir Thomas.

"Trust me," he said soothingly, stopping her in mid-sentence.

He smiled at her in a very friendly way. Rather, she thought with an odd feeling of regret, as her father might have done.

"I promise all will go smoothly, rather more smoothly than this ship at present," he added as the vessel gave another lurch.

"Thank you, my Lord," Justina sighed. She had a wonderful feeling of relief. This was someone who really did understand.

*

Lord Castleton checked the time before he slipped his hunter watch into the pocket of his waistcoat and adjusted its thick gold chain across his midriff.

He wondered how long he would have to wait for Justina's knock on his door.

He picked up a paper from his desk, but did not start

reading. Instead, he castigated himself for deserting the card table this afternoon.

He should not have left Justina with Thomas Watson the way he had. He should have realised she would need protection. After all, it was not her fault he could not stand the man.

Watson had an ancient title, but all the attributes of a cad and a bounder. He had known Thomas's father, Septimus Watson. An upright, punctilious gentleman who had spent his years husbanding the estate and the business that Thomas, if rumour was to be believed, had now squandered.

He realised that somehow he would have to make Watson aware that Justina Mansell was not someone who could be trifled with as he had trifled with other vulnerable girls.

All too clearly he could remember Ariadne's shocked disclosure of a story she had been told by one of Watson's victims, a girl who was her cousin and who was left with a broken heart.

Why, he wondered, was Watson pursuing Justina quite so hard?

Her copper hair, freckled face, deep voice and frank approach made her stand out from the more usual *debutantes*, but he could have sworn that Watson would not in the normal course of events even have noticed her.

At that moment there came a light knock on his door.

"Well done," he exclaimed as he opened it. "I expected you would take much longer to get ready."

"Papa always says a lady should not keep a gentleman waiting," she said, her huge grey eyes shining up at him. "I would have been on time, but I had to ring for the Stewardess to fasten my dress."

There was no hint of flirtatiousness in her voice. It

was a frank statement of fact.

The dress itself was severely simple, its main attraction the colour, a shining pink that should have fought with Justina's hair, but in some pleasing way highlighted the fire in the copper hue.

"You look perfect," he pronounced and her face flushed with pleasure.

Reminding himself that she regarded him as a surrogate father or uncle, Lord Castleton shepherded Justina along the corridor to the Saloon.

The moment they entered, Sir Thomas rose from his table and came forward.

"I think I have the pleasure of Miss Mansell's company this evening," he said and the note of triumph in his voice made Lord Castleton want to punch him. Beside him he felt Justina tense and he controlled himself.

"We emerged from our cabins at the same time. I have no claim on her company, but you cannot be so selfish as to monopolise her when we are so few tonight."

His jovial tone was quite unlike his usual, dispassionate delivery. He looked at the long table that ran down the centre of the room.

"What say we all join together. I am sure the other passengers would appreciate a little feminine company?"

This last remark was addressed to the half dozen or so men already seated at the table.

"What a positively splendid idea," said one.

Two young bucks who had been sitting at the far end, as though they wanted to joke amongst themselves rather than mix with the middle-aged passengers, also rose.

"I say, I think we ought to introduce ourselves."

Tony Price and Bertie Cartwright were both Subalterns on their way to their regiment in India and were delighted to join any party which included Justina.

"I think you will find that Miss Mansell would prefer a more private table," said Sir Thomas, trying to take her arm.

Lord Castleton somehow managed to place his tall, commanding figure in a position that meant Justina was protected from Sir Thomas's approach.

"I say, Miss Mansell, you don't really begrudge us the pleasure of your company?" said one of the Subalterns, holding out a chair for her in the centre of the table.

She smiled gratefully at him as she sat down and the two young men swiftly placed themselves on either side of her. Sir Thomas had no option but to seat himself opposite.

Lord Castleton waited for two other passengers to sit on the same side as Sir Thomas before he placed himself between them and Arthur Wright.

He enjoyed the sight of Justina responding to the two young Officers rather as she would to obstreperous puppies.

She seemed perfectly at ease and managed to ignore Sir Thomas, bad temperedly tapping the table.

Arthur Wright said in a quiet tone that did not carry,

"You are a diplomat of the first water, my Lord."

Lord Castleton said nothing.

"It could have proved an awkward situation for her tonight," Arthur continued. "It will be all right for her now, but I think you have made an enemy."

"He was one already."

The words were out before he could stop them.

Arthur looked at him curiously.

"I think it is going to be an interesting voyage," he said finally.

'Yes,' Lord Castleton told himself, 'it will be most interesting.'

He had meant to spend the journey acquainting himself with his mission, instead he had appointed himself as something between a guard-dog and a careful uncle to a delightful but too-innocent and naïve girl.

Where would it lead?

*

The following day the motion of the ship was still keeping most of the passengers in their cabins, but the sun was shining.

Lord Castleton went up early to the kennels to take Breck for a walk and found Justina already there, playing with an excited Muffin.

Breck was soon released and the two dogs enjoyed themselves together while Lord Castleton and Justina walked them carefully round the upper deck.

Justina was full of eager questions about India and he found himself describing his earlier visits. He was impressed with her intelligence and how interested she was in the culture and history of India.

When they returned the dogs to their kennels, Lord Castleton watched, smiling, as Justina kissed Muffin and told her she would be fine.

"I expect you have papers to study, my Lord?" said Justina as the Steward locked Muffin's kennel.

He wanted very much to suggest that they played cards together again, but knew it was not a sensible proposition.

"Indeed, I do. What plans do you have?"

"I need to check on my maid, Dorcas, and the Arbuthnots. Perhaps there is something I can do for the poor things. And then I want to practice on the piano in the Lounge. It seems days since I was last able to play."

He wished her luck and watched her battle with the pitch of the ship as she made her way down to Second Class and her sick servant.

Back in his cabin he tried to feel grateful that she could be so unselfconscious with him, rather than regretful that she obviously looked on him as someone of her father's generation.

An hour later, he pushed away his papers and gave in to the compulsion that had been growing stronger and stronger as he tried to absorb their contents.

He entered the Lounge and found a chair a little way from the piano.

Justina was playing a Beethoven sonata, one that he knew well. She was so absorbed in her music, she had not noticed him. There was a tricky passage that she played over again and again.

After listening to her for a little while, Lord Castleton walked up to the piano.

"Can I suggest a slightly different fingering?" he said.

She looked up at him, her face alight.

"Please, I have been trying to master this passage and I don't know why I am having such difficulty."

He sat on the piano stool beside her.

"You are crossing over your hands for the chords. I find that keeping my left and right on their natural sides means I am better positioned for the continuation."

He demonstrated.

Justina watched and then copied him.

"Why, that is so much easier!" she cried. "I cannot understand why my teacher preferred the other method."

"Looks more stylish?"

She gave him one of her delightful grins.

"I think you must know him, my Lord. Now, let me see if I can play the sonata from beginning to end."

He moved back to his armchair and listened with great enjoyment to her interpretation of one of his favourite Beethoven pieces.

"Bravo," he applauded at the end.

"Now you must play something," urged Justina.

"I have a better idea. How about a duet?"

"Splendid," agreed Justina.

She riffled through the little pile that sat on the piano and placed some music on the rack.

It was a Schumann piece he used to play with Ariadne. For a moment he hesitated before slipping onto the seat beside Justina.

She held her hands ready and looked at him for the cue to start. Soon they were playing together as though they had done so many times.

Other passengers arrived during the piece and listened appreciatively. The applause at the end was enthusiastic.

"Most pleasurable," said Arthur. "Can we hope for an encore?"

Lord Castleton looked at Justina.

"Do you know this one?" he asked and started another of the duets he and Ariadne had often played together.

Regretfully she shook her head.

"Then, please, play something else yourself," he said and went and sat beside the civil servant.

For a moment it looked as though she would protest, but she gave him a smile and began a Chopin prelude.

As it came to an end in came Sir Thomas.

"Well, well," he said with an open smile. "Miss Mansell, you offer delicious surprises at every turn. Seldom have I heard that piece given such delicacy of touch and interpretation. Please, play again."

Lord Castleton quietly rose and left the Lounge.

Justina looked up at Sir Thomas, pleased at his sincere-sounding praise of her playing.

As before, the sparkle in his brown eyes gave her a feeling of excitement. Dining alone with him was, she knew, unacceptable, but having him appreciate her playing was perfectly allowable. She smiled and began another Chopin piece.

Almost immediately she noticed that Lord Castleton had left the Lounge and her enjoyment in the music evaporated.

At the end of the piece, she closed the piano and rose.

"Enough for today," she said.

She picked up her pile of music and left the Lounge.

Dorcas was no better, but her Stewardess reassured Justina that it was just a matter of waiting for the seas to become calmer.

There were a few more passengers at dinner that evening but not many. Once again there seemed to be general agreement that those present should congregate at the long table.

Justina had gone down to the baggage deck and found the plainest of all of the dresses she had brought, a navy-blue taffeta gown trimmed with white satin.

With her string of pearls around her neck, Justina thought that she looked neat if unexceptional.

Until, that is, she met Lord Castleton in the corridor outside their cabins and saw the admiration in his eyes.

His look awoke the strangest feeling in her breast.

"Miss Mansell," he began. "Every evening you manage to look more beautiful."

She smiled shyly at him, thinking how very elegant he looked in his evening dress, so sophisticated and handsome.

Conversation at the table was very general and Sir Thomas contributed several interesting anecdotes on life in Bombay that had Justina asking him for more.

She left the table at the end of the meal and found her way back to her cabin full of anticipation over reaching India.

But she was enjoying the voyage more and more. She felt that Sir Thomas had to be one of the most exciting men she had met and Lord Castleton one of the nicest and most interesting.

*

It seemed natural to Justina to find Lord Castleton on the kennel deck early the following morning. She greeted him with delight and then found her attention caught by an unfamiliar sight.

"Why, look, my Lord, land!" she cried, gazing over at the port side of the ship.

"It's Cape Finisterre," Lord Castleton informed her. "It is the most westerly point of Europe."

"Have we now left the Bay of Biscay?"

He nodded.

"The seas should ease a little now. It's been blowing so hard, though, that I doubt we shall reach calmer waters until tomorrow."

Nor did they.

Doing her rounds of the seasickness victims, however, Justina found that the Arbuthnots were beginning to feel a little improvement. All three had been able to take a little refreshment.

Dorcas, though, was still in a desperate condition and Justina grew so worried about her that the Stewardess suggested that the Surgeon should be asked to see her.

He came immediately. After examining the maid, he

told Justina that she was one of the unfortunate souls who took a long time to adjust to a ship's motion.

"Rest assured, Miss Mansell, that she will recover. I will provide a sedative that will help her to rest a little more easily."

Still worried but feeling now that everything that could be had been done, Justina returned to First Class.

Almost immediately she encountered Sir Thomas, who insisted she accompany him in some songs.

"As soon as the weather improves, there is bound to be an Entertainments Committee and I shall be asked to contribute a turn to the concert they will organise," he told her.

Sir Thomas hurried off and Justina practised scales until he returned with his music. It was a collection of ballads, most of which Justina recognised.

Sir Thomas had a pleasant baritone and knew the songs by heart. He looked a fine figure as he stood in the curve of the piano, his fair hair immaculately brushed and a scarlet cravat at his throat.

"You will be the star of the show," enthused Justina as he reached the end of his practice recital. "But will there really be a concert?"

"Of course," he said with conviction. "We have to amuse ourselves. And I shall enjoy hearing you perform."

For once he spoke simply without the exaggerated compliments that disturbed Justina.

The evening passed pleasantly with the long table now filling up with more passengers who had gained their sea legs.

Justina welcomed the prospect of calmer seas but, as she enjoyed her dinner, she became aware that a precious part of her day was about to vanish. With the emergence of the Arbuthnots from their cabin, she would no longer be required to exercise Muffin.

She looked down the table at Lord Castleton, deep in conversation with Arthur Wright and realised how much she would miss encountering him at the kennels.

He looked up at that moment and gave her one of his friendly smiles.

If he continued spending most of his time studying papers in his cabin, without their morning walks, she would hardly see him.

*

Next morning she hurried to the kennel deck.

"Ah," remarked Lord Castleton as soon as she appeared. "You are in your Sunday best."

Justina had abandoned the shabby clothes she had been wearing and put on the dark green barathea skirt and jacket with military frogging that had been her outfit for boarding the ship. It was very becoming and she was glad of its warmth in the brisk breeze.

Muffin was whining to be released, but the kennel Steward said they would have to wait until later.

"It's Muster," he explained. "I have to join the rest of the ship's company."

Already they could see crewmen gathering on the main deck below.

"Let's watch," suggested Lord Castleton. "It happens every Sunday morning and is quite a sight."

Justine looked on entranced as more and more men, all smartly dressed, crowded onto the deck until it seemed that there could not be a man left to attend to the sailing of the ship.

"Oh, there will be," Lord Castleton assured her. "But only the very essential men. After the Muster there will be a fire and boat drill. Very reassuring for us passengers."

He smiled at Justina, his deep blue eyes very kind, and once again she felt her heart stop.

"Then we have Divine Service," he added.

"So we will not be able to walk the dogs until much later," Justina murmured, clutching at the rail as she directed her gaze at the now complete ship's company.

"I am afraid not," said Lord Castleton ruefully.

After Divine Service, Justina disappeared, saying she would be back shortly.

Lord Castleton watched her neat little figure hurry off towards the cabin accommodation.

There had been a goodly number of passengers assembled for the Service, and, as they dispersed, he saw Mrs. Arbuthnot and her daughters arrive on deck, followed by Stewards carrying deck chairs.

"Lord Castleton!" Mrs. Arbuthnot waved at him. "Is it not splendid that the wind has given up its force? I have never suffered so much. Faith and Charity, my darling daughters, are also feeling so much better."

The two girls smiled at him, managing to appear at the same time both frail and in good health.

"I am very happy to hear that, madam, and you will be happy to hear that Miss Mansell has been exercising Muffin every day."

"Indeed, I understand that the two of you have been sharing doggy experiences, she with my Muffin, you with your hound, my Lord. It is inestimably kind of you to have looked after poor little Miss Mansell. Alone as she is, since I and the girls have been so confined to our beds, she must have been very grateful for your attentions."

There was a none-too subtle undertone to this remark that made him determined to intervene, but Mrs. Arbuthnot was not yet done.

"Indeed, the whole ship is talking about how close the two of you have become," she continued with a roguish smile. "I am feeling that my role as duenna to dear Justina must be taken up again without delay if she is not to succumb to dangerous gossip. A girl's reputation is so precious, it must not be allowed to be compromised – "

"Madam," intercepted Lord Castleton, infuriated beyond measure. "I cannot imagine who has been suggesting anything of the kind. As you know, I am a friend of Miss Mansell's father. She and I are more than passing acquaintances. I therefore have a duty to keep what you might call the eye of a *paterfamilias* on Miss Mansell. I trust that you will correct any other impression that might be put forward."

He stood rigid with distaste and fixed her with his most baleful look.

"My dear Lord Castleton, please do not upset yourself. Miss Mansell's quite extraordinary ability to withstand conditions that we females with a frailer constitution find quite oversetting, has, of course, made her an object of interest."

"Now that more clement weather has enabled those frailer constitutions to emerge from seclusion, no doubt she will return to being a quite ordinary passenger," he responded repressively.

He was more alarmed at Mrs. Arbuthnot's words than he dared show.

Here he had been trying to protect Justina and it now appeared that he was in danger of compromising her. He had to look to his own situation as well. Better men than he had been accused of compromising a girl's reputation and found themselves trapped into marriage.

"Mama," said Charity. "The only person who has mentioned Justina's friendship with Lord Castleton is Sir

Thomas. I am sure he is mistaken in his conclusions."

"I certainly hope so," Mrs. Arbuthnot said in an unusually sharp voice.

"And you may be assured, Lord Castleton, that I will see that dear little Justina's conduct for the remainder of the voyage will be above comment."

He gave a small bow of acknowledgement and prepared to move on.

"My Lord," Mrs. Arbuthnot called after him. "I would be most grateful if you could be courteous enough to show Faith where the kennels are. She must relieve Justina of the arduous duty of exercising my precious Muffin."

"It sounds as though it would be too arduous for such a recent invalid," he could not resist reposting.

Faith unwrapped herself from her rug and stood. She fluttered her lashes at Lord Castleton.

"It would be so kind of you, my Lord. I quite long for a health-giving stroll in the bracing sea air."

Lord Castleton gave an inward sigh as he realised that not only was refusal impossible, but that he would have to confine himself to working in his cabin for the next few days.

Meanwhile, Justina opened her cabin door and then stood on the threshold realising that there was something very odd. Her nightwear had been neatly hung up, which meant that the Steward had made her bed and cleaned the cabin.

But the bedspread, instead of being neatly arranged, was rucked up.

And the porthole, which Justina had left only slightly ajar, was now wide open. Someone had entered the cabin and made a hasty exit across the bed.

She had been burgled!

CHAPTER FIVE

Justina ran to the cabin door and looked out along the narrow deck. She could see no one. So far she had not noticed anyone pass this way other than the odd member of the crew.

Hastily Justina checked her possessions, starting with her string of pearls and their matching earrings.

As far as she could see everything was there.

She straightened the bedspread. Perhaps the Steward had been interrupted in his cleaning of the cabin.

She had come down to find the tit-bits she had taken away from dinner the previous evening as a treat for Muffin. She opened the drawer where she had left them – and discovered that they were no longer there.

Justina blushed to think that the Steward must have found and removed them. What had he thought? That Justina had not had enough to eat at dinner?

Her face flaming, she slammed the drawer shut and hurriedly left the cabin.

It did not take her more than a glance to see that Lord Castleton was no longer on the main deck where she had left him.

She failed to see Mrs. Arbuthnot and Charity lying on their deck chairs as she turned to go up the companionway to the kennel deck.

So it was a surprise to find Lord Castleton with the two dogs and Faith.

The moment Muffin saw her, she lunged forward, barking in welcome.

She knelt to the little dog and allowed her to lick her face. Then she picked up the lead and returned it to Faith.

"I am so pleased to see you up and about again," she said. "I hope your mother and sister are as well? Muffin will be delighted to have you all back."

Since it was obvious that the dog would prefer to be with Justina rather than Faith, her comment was met with stony silence.

Breck tried to sniff at Muffin and Faith pulled the little dog away, her nose wrinkling in distaste.

"Please, my Lord, will you keep your dog under control?" she implored, glancing demurely up at him. "I am sure you find his attentions towards Muffin as embarrassing as I do."

Lord Castleton brought Breck to heel and replied, poker faced.

"I suggest in that case, Miss Arbuthnot, you walk that way with your dog and I take mine the other side of the deck."

Faith, obviously realising that she had made it impossible to share the walk with Lord Castleton, looked daggers at Justina. Trying to recover, she said,

"It will not take me long to give Muffin her walk, my Lord, then perhaps I may join you and your dog?"

Justina would have liked to join them, but knew that it would not be polite. Nor had Lord Castleton seemed at all welcoming to her. He had only given a stiff little nod as she came onto the deck.

"Would you like some company?" she asked Faith.

"I am fine," Faith snapped, dragging a reluctant

Muffin away from Justina. "But I am sure Mama would like you to say hallo, she is on the deck below."

Stifling a sigh, Justina went to find Mrs. Arbuthnot.

Then had to endure a lecture over her loose behaviour in allowing Lord Castleton to monopolise her company.

Justina, incensed, tried to tell her that she had seen very little of his Lordship, but it was hopeless. Mrs. Arbuthnot made her feel at fault for not having succumbed to seasickness, as every other sensitive female had.

"Mrs. Arbuthnnot," Justina started, scarlet with anger.

"Not a word, Justina, I beg of you. Merely consider what your aunt would say if she heard of your conduct."

Justina wanted to say that her aunt was at least fair and would allow her to correct a mistaken impression, but courtesy held her silent.

Full of rage, she strode to the lounge and gave a storming performance of a Liszt piece, performing the passages she normally stumbled over with great élan.

There was a little spurt of applause from a couple sitting with a pre-lunch drink as she finished and Justina saw that Arthur Wright had been joined by his wife, Patience, a large woman with white hair arranged in a plait around her head and a sensible-looking countenance.

"So this is the Miss Mansell I have heard so much about," said Mrs. Wright with a friendly smile. "I am so pleased to meet you at last."

"And I am you," replied Justina. "It is a great relief to me that I am no longer the only woman not suffering from *mal de mer.* I thought I was lucky, now it seems that I have proved to be unfeminine."

"My dear, who has been saying such an unkind thing to you?" Patience looked distressed.

"Sheer jealousy," said her husband. "Take no notice, Miss Mansell."

"Come and sit down and tell me all about it," invited Patience with a sympathetic smile.

Patience Wright was so warm and sensible, it was rather like talking with her mother, except that she suspected she had a much better grasp of how the world worked.

Justina was eager to listen to anything this sage counsellor might propose.

By the time they walked into lunch, Justina had formed a plan of campaign to rescue her position as far as the Arbuthnots were concerned.

Sitting at the small table with them, she glanced longingly at the long table in the middle of the Saloon, now more than half full of passengers chatting happily.

Sir Thomas was there, talking in a desultory manner, but Lord Castleton never appeared.

Throughout lunch, Justina sat with eyes cast down and allowed Mrs. Arbuthnot to talk freely about the travails she and her daughters had untaken.

Oh, how she missed the interesting conversation there had been at the general table, but she said nothing.

She did not miss, however, the glances that Tony and Bertie threw her way.

"Please," she said prettily to Mrs. Arbuthnot at the end of the meal. "May I introduce Faith and Charity to two Subalterns I have met? I thought perhaps we might make up a game of deck quoits."

She had only a hazy idea of what would be involved, but trusted that one of the others would be better informed.

It proved an excellent move. Tony and Bertie were as delighted to meet Faith and Charity as the girls were to be introduced to them. Tony proved to know all about deck quoits.

They set up the little pole and began to throw the rope circles.

Justina knew it was something she would be very good at, as they played a similar game at home and she had an exceedingly good eye. So good an eye, in fact, that she was able to ensure her throws went near but never over the pole.

They had not been playing long before Sir Thomas came by. Immediately he wanted to join in.

"Let us form teams," he proposed. Faith and Charity clapped their hands and exclaimed that it was a wonderful idea.

"Miss Mansell and I will be one team," he continued. "We have enjoyed time together ever since we sailed," he added to Justina's discomfiture.

Faith gave Charity a look, but before she could say anything, Tony had claimed her and Bertie said how delighted he would be if Charity partnered him.

Justina found it difficult to concentrate and she realised that she was actually waiting to see if a tall, elegant figure was among the passengers who were strolling along the deck in the sun.

Dinner that night was an uncomfortable affair for her.

Faith and Charity were full of the games they had played that afternoon. Faith, though, bemoaned the fact that Lord Castleton had not been one of the players.

"He is the most charming of gentlemen," she said with a huge sigh and directed a beaming smile towards the table where he sat alone.

Lord Castleton did not appear to notice her attentions as he was reading papers and soon collected them together and disappeared.

Justina could not believe that he had not so much as glanced in her direction.

Had she imagined their easy relationship? If it had ever existed, it now seemed to have evaporated.

"We reach Gibraltar tomorrow," Mrs. Arbuthnot announced with satisfaction. "Such an opportunity for shopping, girls. We shall go ashore." After a moment she added, "Will you come with us, Justina?"

"Please, forgive me, Mrs. Arbuthnot, but I still have a headache. I think it would be best if I spent the day quietly in my cabin."

At that moment Sir Thomas stopped at their table.

"Dear lady, what a pleasure it is to see you and your beautiful daughters with us once again. Can I hope that you will allow me to return your hospitality of the first night? I would be so delighted if you would all join me for dinner."

Mrs. Arbuthnot accepted the invitation with alacrity.

Sir Thomas bowed to her and it seemed to Justina that he tried to catch her glance, but she resolutely kept her eyes demurely fixed on her plate.

The voyage, which had seemed so exciting only a day ago, had lost all its attractions for her.

*

Despite her depression, the next morning Justina found herself standing on deck witnessing their arrival at Gibraltar.

There was a four-hour stay in port while fuel and supplies were taken aboard and horse drawn carriages awaited the passengers who wished to visit the town, a short distance from the dock.

Looming over both town and harbour was the famous grey limestone rock.

Soldiers were marching to the beat of a band. It was an English sound such as she had heard in Surrey, but she also saw turbaned Moors and Arabs dressed in loose grey garments and women in Spanish attire, lace suspended from high combs in their dark hair.

The air was sweet with unknown aromas. Sub-tropical trees clustered in gardens belonging to the houses she could see arranged around the port.

She could see shops and the thought came to her that maybe she could find a gift there to take to her brother. Perhaps a humidor or some cigars.

She ran back to her cabin and threw a wrap over her starched blouse and linen skirt. Winter clothes could now be left behind.

Soon she was amongst the shops, charmed by the range of goods on offer and greatly tempted by the lace mantillas.

"The señorita is from the ship?" asked the shopkeeper. "Perhaps need a fancy dress?"

Fancy dress? Dimly Justina remembered someone saying that there was usually a night during the voyage when passengers organised such an evening. She had not brought anything to wear at such an occasion.

"Come and see how it would look, señorita," urged the shopkeeper and took her through a bead curtain into an area at the back of the shop where there was a large mirror. "My wife will help you."

There was a pile of lace mantillas on a table at the back of the area and she reached for the black one that lay on top.

At that moment, from the main part of the shop, came the sound of familiar voices.

"She has *all* the men after her, Mama," whimpered Faith.

"I can't understand why, she isn't at all pretty," moaned Charity discontentedly. "She's a *nothing*."

"And at dinner this evening Sir Thomas will address himself only to her," protested Faith. "Just as he did at deck quoits yesterday afternoon. We've only been asked to join his table because he cannot ask her on her own."

Justina looked at her reflection in the mirror with wide appalled eyes.

It was terrible to have Faith and Charity speak so unkindly. Equally unsettling was to have it suggested that Sir Thomas was only interested in her.

For the first time she wondered whether it was possible that his admiration was serious. Until now she had assumed he was merely passing the voyage by flirting with her. She wished she had quizzed her sisters over how their suitors had behaved when they first met.

Justina certainly was *not* in love with Sir Thomas, but there was no doubt she was attracted to him. She thought again with a sinking heart of Mrs. Arbuthnot telling him how rich her father was, information she had had no opportunity to correct.

Then she remembered with relief that she had been told Sir Thomas was very wealthy himself. Her non-existent fortune could mean nothing to him.

For an instant she wondered what it would be like to be married to Sir Thomas. She would have a great house of her own and her mother and father would undoubtedly be delighted. They would consider she had done extremely well.

But, she thought, would she come to love Sir Thomas as Vicky loved Edward?

As the mantilla was arranged over the comb, Justina heard Mrs. Arbuthnot's voice.

"Girls, girls! I can understand your chagrin. You are both so much more attractive than poor Justina. But, remember, for the last four days she has been the only girl not confined to her cabin. Men in a desert, you know! Now things are very different and I think you will find that her charms, such as they are, will be completely overshadowed by those of my lovely daughters."

"Someone who doesn't appear to be charmed by Justina is Lord Castleton," added Faith suddenly. "Despite what Sir Thomas told us. When I was exercising Muffin with him, he quite cut her dead."

She gave an excited little laugh while Justina felt as though cold water had been poured over her.

Then Faith continued,

"Mama, if you allow Sir Thomas to attach himself to Justina, I would have a clear field with Lord Castleton."

"What a common way you have of putting things," pouted Charity. "Do let us leave, I see nothing here to interest us."

Justina found she was trembling. How could they talk in such a way?

She no longer cared to find a gift for Peter. There would be other ports where she could look for something, now she wanted to return to the ship.

She walked quickly back, scanning the street in case the Arbuthnots were still around. However, it seemed they had for the moment vanished and Justina climbed on board with relief.

As she passed the company office on the main deck, she heard a passenger complaining loudly that there had been a thief in her cabin.

"No, nothing valuable was taken," she said in response to the Officer's questions. "Only some fruit, a gift from friends."

Remembering her impression that her cabin had been invaded by an intruder, Justina lingered to hear more.

"Did you lock your cabin door?" asked the Officer.

"I think so," replied the passenger. "But perhaps I didn't."

*

When the ship sailed from Gibraltar, the sea was calm and the air warm. The dining Saloon was full of happy passengers that evening and there was an expectant atmosphere.

Justina wore her pink dress and made sure that the Arbuthnots were already seated at Sir Thomas's table before she arrived to make up the party.

Lord Castleton was, as usual, at his solitary table only yards away. As the Steward held out the chair for Justina, she caught his glance.

Forgetting the change in their relationship, she gave him a warm smile, which faded as he merely dipped his head in a cool acknowledgement of her presence.

An icy hand seemed to clutch at her heart as she slipped into her seat and tried to respond warmly to Sir Thomas's greeting.

All she could think of, however, was that her relationship with Lord Castleton, for some reason that she could not understand, was no more.

It was not long before he gathered up his papers and left the Saloon. At least she no longer had to view his profile and regret the fun they had had together.

Justina told herself it was useless to look back. She tried to relax and enjoy herself. The food was excellent and Sir Thomas had ordered a pleasant wine.

Not used to alcohol, Justina only sipped at her glass. Faith and Charity were not so abstemious and soon required theirs to be refilled.

Justina sat quietly. Sir Thomas tried to coax her into conversation, but she responded with no more than the odd word, which, strangely, seemed to encourage him to greater efforts.

Then, at the end of the meal, it was announced that dancing was to take place in the Lounge.

The chairs had all been moved back and a carpet removed from a section of polished floor. A pianist was playing a *Sir Roger de Coverly* and passengers were already enjoying themselves on the floor.

Sir Thomas found them places at a small table, ordered some refreshing drinks and asked Mrs. Arbuthnot to dance.

Admiring his manners, Justina watched the two of them perform in a stately manner.

"How I wish I could see Lord Castleton," sighed Faith, craning her neck in case she could discover him in a corner.

Charity gave a wave to the two young Subalterns as they came into the Lounge, laughing together.

"I say, what luck," Tony said.

"Beauties waiting for us," agreed Bertie, stroking his moustache.

"You may not be the ones we are waiting for," giggled Charity.

Faith and Charity appeared delighted to joke with them and quite soon Sir Thomas brought Mrs. Arbuthnot back and asked Justina to dance a waltz.

For a few moments Justina enjoyed the feel of Sir Thomas's strong arm around her waist.

But as he guided her skilfully into the rhythm of the dance, accompanied by the steady throb of the ship's engines, he grasped her more tightly and began to murmur how beautiful she was looking.

"You are the loveliest woman in the room," he whispered into her ear. "You have no idea how you make me feel. It is as if I am a young man again."

Justina did not know how to respond, so she smiled slightly and said nothing.

"Your looks can drive a man mad," added Sir Thomas, holding her ever more tightly as he twirled her round.

She tried not to think how much more she would have enjoyed dancing with Lord Castleton. She was sure he would never embarrass her in this way.

"I could travel several thousand miles without meeting a girl as attractive and stimulating as you, do you know that?"

"Sir Thomas," protested Justina, now alarmed that the situation was developing beyond her control.

"Ah, you are such an innocent," he murmured. "Can I help it if you fire me to say these words to you?"

As the dance came to an end, Sir Thomas enquired,

"Shall we go on deck? The moon will be reflected in the water in a most romantic way."

"You are – very kind," Justina stammered, "but my wretched headache – is back. I will retire."

Not waiting for a response, she moved over to the Arbuthnots and wished them goodnight and then heard Sir Thomas say that he would accompany her to her cabin in case she felt faint.

"Thank you, sir, but it will not be necessary."

It was no use.

Sir Thomas gripped her elbow and steered her out of the lounge.

Justina said nothing and was immensely relieved that Sir Thomas held back from offering yet more of the compliments she found so difficult to cope with.

She unlocked the door of her cabin and turned to thank him for his courtesy and wish him goodnight.

Then she was horrified to find herself propelled into the cabin.

Sir Thomas's foot kicked the door closed, his arms

held her close and his eager mouth found hers.

Vainly, she attempted to free herself.

The more she struggled, the stronger became his grip.

His mouth seemed to devour hers. He held her head and removed his lips just far enough to say,

"God, you are divine. An innocent wild rose is what you are and you are mine!"

Before she could recover her breath enough to scream, his mouth once more crunched down on hers. His strong body pressed more insistently against hers.

Feeling that she was drowning, Justina tried to kick out, but her long skirt prevented her from landing a useful blow and she failed to dislodge his hold.

Then she found herself pushed onto the bed with Sir Thomas lying on top of her.

Justina struggled more and more desperately and at last managed to cry out.

Suddenly the cabin door opened.

"*Miss Mansell*!" came Mrs. Arbuthnot's outraged voice. "*Sir Thomas*!"

With a groan he released Justina and rose, running a hand through his dishevelled hair and pulling down his waistcoat.

"I came to reassure myself that Justina was not succumbing to some ailment," snapped Mrs. Arbuthnot. "Instead I enter upon a scene that would do justice to a house of ill repute. I can only assume, Sir Thomas, that you are engaged to Miss Mansell."

Sir Thomas seemed taken aback.

Justina lay for a moment gathering her composure before she struggled up and attempted to smooth down the silk of her dress.

"No," she called in a small voice that did not carry and

was quickly covered by Sir Thomas speaking in a loud and definite tone that seemed to defy anybody to disagree with him.

"Indeed, Mrs. Arbuthnot, I have just asked Miss Mansell to take pity on me and promise to be my bride."

His hand grasped Justina's and his thumb caressed the back of her hand in a gentle gesture that was quite different from his violent kisses.

She grew a little calmer. Maybe the way he had pounced upon her had been the result of alcohol as he had drunk a great deal during the evening, and maybe he was now a little more sober. He certainly seemed to be more caring.

"Indeed?" said Mrs. Arbuthnot with a sharp look at Sir Thomas. "Well, Justina, what a lucky girl you are!"

"But – " Justina started.

Mrs. Arbuthnot enfolded her in her arms, preventing her from continuing.

"Darling child, I am so happy for you. Sir Thomas is such a catch! Your parents, oh, your parents will be so delighted and so will the dear Viscountess. Fancy, not five days out of Southampton and you have attached the most eligible bachelor on board! And you, Sir Thomas, have caught the most desirable of all the girls, apart, of course, from my lovely daughters."

"Mrs. Arbuthnot," she tried again. "There is some – "

Once more she was interrupted.

"What is going on here?"

In the doorway stood Lord Castleton.

"I was asleep but I thought I heard someone cry out."

He wore a handsome silk dressing gown over striped pyjamas. It was obvious that he had risen from his bed. His hair was disarranged and he looked anxious.

"Miss Mansell, are you all right?"

"Miss Mansell has just announced that she is engaged to Sir Thomas," gushed Mrs. Arbuthnot inaccurately but triumphantly. "Isn't that the most enchanting news you have ever heard? A shipboard romance, no less."

Sir Thomas put his arm around Justina's shoulders, a touch that made her shiver for a reason she could not identify.

"Miss Mansell has made me the happiest of men," he said, his voice clear and confident.

Lord Castleton looked stunned.

"Miss Mansell, is this true?"

Justina looked up at Sir Thomas, who smiled at her, his teeth very white.

"Why else would I be in this cabin?" he volunteered.

"Indeed, I as Justina's chaperone, would never otherwise allow it," Mrs. Arbuthnot declared.

"Miss Mansell?" Lord Castleton queried, an eyebrow raised in enquiry.

Justina felt helpless.

If she denied the engagement, Lord Castleton would want to know why she had allowed Sir Thomas into her cabin.

Would he believe she had had no choice?

Moreover, it was true that Sir Thomas was most attractive and an eligible bachelor. He seemed enamoured with her and Mrs. Arbuthnot was quite right, her parents would be delighted.

A fiancé who was handsome, rich and well-born.

What more could she want?

She tried to smile at Lord Castleton.

"It has all happened so quickly," she whispered.

"I see."

Lord Castleton looked as though he did not see, but could not argue the matter.

"Watson, you are a fortunate man and I congratulate you. I trust you will both be very happy. I wish you all goodnight," he said and left.

Justina sank down on the bed.

But Sir Thomas lifted her up and placed a light kiss on her mouth that was so much gentler than the throbbing passion he had shown earlier.

"You are the most beautiful of girls and I am, indeed, the happiest of men," he whispered in her ear. "We will talk more tomorrow."

"Oh, yes," fluttered Mrs. Arbuthnot. "If I know Sir Thomas, he will be all eagerness to draw you into a corner and conduct a lovey-dovey conversation at the earliest opportunity. Goodnight, my dearest Justina. Oh, how excited the girls will be when I tell them."

Still twittering, she shepherded Sir Thomas out of the cabin.

Left alone at last, Justina collapsed onto her bed in a torrent of tears.

How had it happened?

How had she become engaged to Sir Thomas Watson?

There were only two things she could be certain of. One was that her parents would be delighted, the other was that the only man in the world she loved was the one in the cabin next door.

When she had seen Lord Castleton's look of surprise as he was told of the engagement, she knew that if only he had been her fiancé she would indeed be the happiest of women.

As it was, she was the unhappiest.

What was she to do?

CHAPTER SIX

Lord Castleton woke with a feeling of doom hanging over him.

It took him a little time to identify the reason.

Then he remembered the scene he had interrupted in the next door cabin.

As he shaved, he reflected that there was something distinctly fishy about the situation. Ariadne, he thought, would have been quick to tell him that a man such as Thomas Watson could not be trusted and that no young girl should be allowed to link her future to his.

He rinsed the last of the soap from his face and remembered how Justina had confided that her parents were expecting her to make a good match and that they would be very disappointed if her Indian adventure did not produce a husband.

Well, she had not had to wait to reach the Subcontinent to make what the world would declare an ideal engagement.

Except if it turned out to be true that Watson had lost all his money. Was that his reason for the engagement? Did he expect to recoup his fortunes through marriage?

No doubt Justina would bring a respectable dowry to her husband.

He curled his lip. Marrying for money would fit in with his opinion of the man.

And what of her?

The idea that Justina had fallen in love with Watson's dubious charms was somehow offensive.

He shrugged his shoulders into a dark blue blazer, flicked some fluff off his white trousers and decided the matter required careful thought, best carried out whilst exercising Breck.

As he closed and locked his cabin door, he found Justina was doing the same with hers.

"Good morning, Miss Mansell," he greeted her in a determinedly cheerful voice. "I trust you had a restful night after all the excitement?"

"I am fine," she murmured.

He was shocked at the change in her.

Gone was the air of eagerness that had been such a distinctive feature, the light in the eyes that announced here was someone who enjoyed life. Instead she appeared to be walking in a dream that was more of a nightmare.

He made up his mind.

"I am going to exercise Breck, why not come with me and let Muffin have the fun of meeting up with her friend again?" he suggested. "I am taking a ball with me, the sea is so calm now I feel it will be possible to allow Breck a little fun."

She flinched, as though fun was something she could not contemplate.

"Come on, the sun is shining." He held out a hand. "No one will see us, it's too early and Breck and Muffin are the only dogs up there anyway."

Justina suddenly smiled, it was like sunlight breaking through dark clouds.

"Why not?"

"Sea air is so invigorating," he mused as they emerged

onto the upper deck.

All around them was the deep blue of the Mediterranean and overhead a sun that blazed brightly and soon would be afire with heat.

Justina took out an ecstatic dog and allowed her face to be licked all over.

Lord Castleton brought out Breck and soon both dogs were exchanging greetings and happily circling each other.

Some of Justina's colour came back and also, it seemed to Lord Castleton, a little of her zest for life.

Finally the dogs were returned to their kennels and the Steward thanked.

As they started to leave the upper deck, Lord Castleton decided that he had to say something. Now, if ever, was the time to capitalise on her view of him as a member of her father's generation.

"Miss Mansell," he started, holding open the door to the companionway. "I have to refer to last night. I flatter myself that we have achieved a friendship whereby I can, perhaps, stand in as something of a surrogate uncle."

A curious expression flitted across her face.

He continued,

"In that capacity and as a long standing friend of your father's, I feel in some way responsible for you on this ship. I fear that you do not seem as happy as a newly engaged young lady should be. If there is anything I can do to help rectify the situation, I hope you will tell me."

For a moment he thought she would confide in him, then she said stiffly,

"Lord Castleton, there is nothing wrong. My relationship with Sir Thomas, well, it has been rather sudden, that is all."

She gave a huge gulp on the last words and fled down

the companionway.

He watched her go, feeling he had made a bad fist of it.

More than ever he was convinced that Justina had somehow been forced into a situation she did not welcome.

He had failed with her and he recognised that there was no point in talking to Mrs. Arbuthnot. She was a silly woman who could only see the engagement as desirable.

The only other person he could tackle was Watson, the last one he wanted to have anything to do with.

It took some time to track the man down but, around ten o'clock, Lord Castleton found him in the otherwise deserted smoking room, dragging on a cigar, a large brandy in front of him.

"Come to congratulate me again, have you, Castleton?" he crowed.

"Not exactly, Watson. As you know, I am a friend of Lord Mansell's and therefore feel some responsibility for Miss Mansell."

"Indeed? My impression was that it was something else you felt for Miss Mansell," Sir Thomas sneered.

Lord Castleton took a deep breath and tried to maintain his calm.

"Last night I received the definite impression that all was not as it should have been. You may well have felt pressured into a situation that in the cold light of day you might regret."

"Look here, has Justina, Miss Mansell, been saying anything to you?" Sir Thomas asked angrily.

Now Lord Castleton was certain there was something wrong about this engagement.

"Nothing," he replied shortly. "I merely want to point out that at present only four people know about this situation, you and Miss Mansell, Mrs. Arbuthnot and myself. It would not be difficult for us to forget anything has happened and you would be free to pursue, well, to pursue whatever other interests you may have in mind."

A puff of cigar smoke was blown in his face.

"I have to tell you, Castleton, that both Miss Mansell and I are happy with our engagement. Once before you did me out of happiness and you are not going to do it again."

"What on earth do you mean?" Lord Castleton was genuinely taken aback.

"Don't say you have forgotten snatching Ariadne Somerset from under my nose?" Sir Thomas gestured to a Steward to refill his glass.

"Don't be so ridiculous."

The other man's eyes narrowed.

"How dare you call me ridiculous."

"You had no more chance of engaging Ariadne's affections than I have of, well, of navigating this ship."

Lord Castleton was incensed at the man's presumption.

Sir Thomas extinguished the remains of his cigar, jabbing the stub into the ashtray in a pent-up fury.

"You always had too much pride, Castleton. You cannot stand it that Miss Mansell prefers me to you." He fumbled for his cigar case. "Let me warn you, you interfering cad. If you persuade Miss Mansell to break off this engagement, I will see her branded a heartless minx. The sort of girl who leads a man on and then leaves him in the lurch. That, I think, would not suit either you or her."

Lord Castleton stood.

There was no reasoning with the man and he realised, with a sinking heart, that he had made matters worse. If Watson had been regretting the engagement before he arrived, he certainly was not now.

"I hope Miss Mansell is genuinely happy at the prospect of becoming Lady Watson," he said slowly. "But if you harm her in any way, let me warn you that there are no lengths to which I will not go to see you damned in hell!"

He turned and stalked off.

"Huh!" came a triumphant exclamation from behind him. "Beaten you, haven't I?"

Lord Castleton sought the fresh air outside.

He stood holding the rail of the promenade deck and taking deep breaths, trying to regain his composure.

He faced the fact that Watson had put one issue to rights.

He, Marcus Castleton, had fallen in love with a girl some fifteen years younger than himself, who regarded him as nothing more than a friend of her father.

*

After leaving Lord Castleton, Justina had breakfast in the Saloon.

The idea of asking for it in her cabin was impossible. In there she could only think of the way Sir Thomas had pressed his attentions on her the previous night.

Her mouth was still bruised from the ferocity of his kisses.

She tried to remember his more tender approach after Mrs. Arbuthnot had disturbed them.

The more she tried, the more she realised that exercising the dogs with Lord Castleton had made it clear to her that he was the man she loved. Spending even a short time with him was a joy.

The tone of his voice, the long, elegant hands throwing the ball for the dogs, the way his eyes crinkled as he smiled at something she had said. The kindness in his eyes as he looked at her.

But that kindness was, of course, due to his feeling that he owed something to his friendship with her father.

That had been glaringly obvious from the way that he had spoken to her about her engagement to Sir Thomas.

Justina grew more and more depressed.

She entered the Saloon and looked around, hoping very much that Sir Thomas would not have altered his usual routine.

There was no Sir Thomas and no Arbuthnots, but Arthur was seated at the long table and Justina joined him with a sense of relief. For a short while she could enjoy hearing more about his experiences in India.

Afterwards, though, she felt a sense of dislocation.

What was now to happen with the time she had planned to spend with her brother? Would Sir Thomas insist she remain in Bombay rather than travel across almost half of India to where Peter was stationed in the Central Provinces?

Surely even though they were only engaged, she would be allowed to join a member of her family?

Out on the Promenade deck, Justina could see the Arbuthnots enjoying the sun on their deck chairs. Quietly fetching one of the books she had borrowed from the library, Justina found a quiet spot far away from Mrs. Arbuthnot and her daughters.

A little while later Sir Thomas found her.

"Well, well, my little fiancée," he began and gave her a wide smile. "Shall we promenade, my dear Justina?"

There was little she could do other than join him in circling the deck, but at least she was able to clutch the book to her chest as they walked, so that he was unable to link his arm with hers.

"I hope," he stated confidently, "that you are filled with the same joy as I myself feel at the unexpected events of last night."

She had not anticipated so straightforward an approach. His manner was frank and open and for the first time she felt she might be able to trust him.

"You took me by surprise," she mumbled slowly.

"I felt that was probably the case. Your beauty quite overcame my most gentlemanly instincts. You must be aware of the effect you have on me."

Justina blushed.

"If Mrs. Arbuthnot had not arrived in such a precipitous manner, I should have asked you to be my wife. Ever since I saw you looking so incredibly lovely in that grey dress on the first night, I have thought of nothing but you. I have wished to spend every minute of the voyage with you, to tell you of the effect your nearness has on my body."

Justina moved away from him. She was not used to any man speaking to her like this. It was exciting, disturbing even, but also, she could not help but feel, somewhat frightening. Again she remembered how he had forced himself upon her.

"As it was," he went on smoothly as though he had not noticed her slight withdrawal. "Mrs. Arbuthnot pre-empted the presentation of my humble suit. You must never feel that anything else was ever my intention."

He paused, put out a hand and brought her to a stop. His expression was full of intensity.

"In saying you will be my wife, you have fulfilled my wildest hopes."

Justina swallowed hard and her heart sank.

He had given her no opportunity to express the wish to be given a little time to consider whether she really wished to be engaged to him.

He was so very handsome, so debonair and carried himself so well. Any girl should be wild with excitement that he wanted her to be his wife.

Mrs. Arbuthnot had declared he was the most eligible of bachelors. Married to Sir Thomas Watson, she would be rich, secure and able to fulfil all her ambitions.

Mama and Papa would be free from worrying about her future. She would run her own household and make Sir Thomas's life comfortable.

She should be exultant.

He was waiting for her to say something.

What could she say?

That she could never be happy married to him because he was not Lord Castleton?

"You are very kind, sir," she said in a small voice. "As you say, it has all happened so very quickly. I-I need a little time to adjust."

An ugly expression came over his face and he gripped her arm.

At that moment a couple of girls rushed up.

"Miss Mansell, is it not? And Sir Thomas Watson?" They gazed up at him with admiration in their eyes. "We are part of the Entertainment's Committee. It has just been formed. There is to be a concert. Do say you will perform? We have heard Miss Mansell is such a good pianist and that you, Sir Thomas, sing divinely. You must, we insist you must – *do say yes*."

"Why, of course we will," Sir Thomas agreed immediately.

"And will you come with us now? We are to have a rehearsal in the Lounge."

Justina was not sorry to have her tête-à-tête with Sir

Thomas interrupted. And he looked pleased to be applied to in such an enthusiastic way.

As they made their way off the Promenade Deck, Sir Thomas announced that he must collect his music and left her. Justina, too, went to collect hers.

Returning and attempting to open the Lounge door, the collection of sheets slipped out of her grasp and fell on the floor.

She bent to pick it up.

"Let me help you," came a voice and there was Lord Castleton.

"Oh, thank you," gasped Justina, taking the music from him.

He put a hand beneath her elbow to help her rise and his touch was like fire.

"Are you going in to practice again?"

Justina found herself telling him about the concert.

"They are looking for volunteers."

From somewhere unexpected courage arose and she continued,

"Could we, perhaps, perform the Schumann duet we played the other day?"

For a moment he stood without speaking and an unidentifiable wave of emotion washed through her. It was as though her bones were melting and the blood in her veins was sinking to the soles of her feet.

Then, in an indifferent voice, he replied,

"I think not, Miss Mansell. There will be more than sufficient talent to entertain those aboard. I shall not be required. Good day to you."

He strode off, leaving Justina looking despairingly after him.

There was no hope, of course, that he could ever have felt for her what she now knew she felt for him, but she had hoped it would be possible for them to remain friends.

"Waiting for me, that's a good girl," trumpeted Sir Thomas, arriving with a music case under his arm.

He gripped her elbow possessively and ushered her into the Lounge.

There, two commanding women had taken charge.

They announced themselves as highly experienced travellers and that a happy ship was one where everyone was kept occupied.

Justina was prevailed upon to perform a Chopin Mazurka.

"Something lively is ideal," said Mrs. Russell, one of the commanding women.

After the last of the passengers had performed, they were told,

"You are all very talented but I hope that you will all practice hard before the actual night. We will inform you of the running order and then we shall have a proper rehearsal."

It all helped Justina put behind her the unfortunate encounter with Lord Castleton.

At lunch Faith was sulking.

"I had to exercise Muffin all on my own this morning," she moaned. "Lord Castleton was nowhere about."

"You should have let me accompany you, instead of saying you were perfectly happy on your own," put in Charity, sounding righteous.

"Now, girls," intervened Mrs. Arbuthnot. "Why not find Lord Castleton, Faith, my dear, and suggest that tomorrow you go together? I am sure he would welcome some company."

Justina sat silent, relieved to be without the company

of Sir Thomas for a while.

"Now, Justina, my dear, we shall, of course, dine with your fiancé this evening. Will you want to announce your engagement? I am sure I would in your place, such a *coup*, the whole ship will be a-flutter."

Justina looked at her in astonishment.

"I cannot possibly announce any engagement until my father has given his consent. Sir Thomas must write to him and ask for my hand."

Mrs Arbuthnot looked agitated.

"Do you really think that is necessary? I mean, he certainly will not oppose so advantageous a match."

Justina knew exactly what to say.

"My aunt, the Viscountess, would think any other way of behaving would not be at all *comme-il-faut*. She would insist we followed the proper paths."

"Oh, dear Lady Elder, of course, of course. Well, girls, we shall have to keep our delicious little secret for a while longer, it seems."

"Just as well, otherwise Justina would get all the attention," said Charity.

"But it would remove her from the roll call of eligible girls," protested Faith

Justina gave a great sigh.

When the weather had been rough and the ship battling against the elements, the voyage had promised excitement and unexpected pleasures, with all the anticipated delights of India at its finish.

Now, for her, all had been ruined.

CHAPTER SEVEN

After luncheon Sir Thomas persuaded Justina to take another turn around the deck with him.

When she told him that no engagement could be announced until he had applied to her father for her hand in marriage, he was not pleased.

"This is preposterous," he exclaimed. "You are mine and I want the whole world and certainly this ship to know about it."

"My father would never countenance such a way of proceeding," responded Justina firmly.

If only she could stave off an official announcement of their engagement, there was the faint possibility that Sir Thomas might find someone else more to his liking.

Sir Thomas's face darkened suddenly.

"Who has told you our engagement should not be immediately announced," he snorted and caught hold of her arm in his strong grip.

Justina gasped in pain.

"You are hurting me," she protested.

A couple of passengers were approaching and he immediately released her.

"I am sorry, but I need you to answer my question. Who told you to say our engagement should not be announced immediately? And don't tell me it was Mrs. Arbuthnot."

"No, indeed, it was *I* who said it to *her*. Though why you should be so convinced it was her, I do not understand. After all, she is my chaperone. You cannot think," she went on, becoming indignant, "that any well brought up girl would announce that she was engaged *before* her father had given his consent?"

He was silent for several minutes, looking at her, his eyes narrowed, one hand massaging the fist that the other had formed.

"Did you not think that you would have to write to Papa?" Justina added. She wanted to ask him, 'How do you think a gentleman normally behaves?' but felt she had done enough to make it plain to him.

"Of course I am writing to your father," he came back smoothly, letting his hands fall to his side. "I am fully aware of my duty. There are, after all, a number of formalities to be gone through."

Only later did Justina wonder what he meant by this.

"And no doubt you, too, will be writing to express your delight at receiving my offer."

Justina had agonised already over the letter she had to write, but so far she had not managed to put pen to paper.

"It will be posted in Malta," she said slowly. "I believe we call in there in a few days time."

He nodded.

"We put into Valletta, the Capital. It is a beautiful place and I shall look forward to showing you around."

He hesitated a moment and then said,

"I cannot imagine that letters sent from Malta would receive a reply until some time after we land in Bombay."

"No," Justina agreed, trying to sound sad.

"However," Sir Thomas resumed, slipping a hand underneath her elbow and guiding her into continuing their walk. "We shall still be engaged. Nothing can change that. We shall dine together and dance together in the evenings. During the daytime we shall be able to promenade."

He brought out a watch from a pocket in his blazer.

"However, shortly I am due to play whist. You may have wondered what I am doing when not on the deck or in the Lounge?"

It had not occurred to Justina to speculate about how Sir Thomas spent his time. She realised now that she had never looked for his companionship.

"I am in the top rank of whist players and spend many pleasant hours at the card table. If I do not always dance attendance on you, you are not to assume that I am with other girls."

Justina's first thought was relief that he would not be insisting on her company the whole time. Then she reflected how strange it would be to suspect that the man who said he loved her so passionately could be spending time with another girl.

"It might be natural for you to think that as there are some very attractive females emerging now that the sea has calmed down," Sir Thomas added, lifting his yachting cap to a girl in her early twenties on the deck. "But none so beautiful as you, my dearest Justina. You are the light of my life and I am sure that others will soon realise that you are mine."

It should have been delightful to hear such compliments, but Sir Thomas spoke so passionately that Justina felt frightened.

He looked again at his watch.

"Now I have to leave you, but only until dinner. You will perhaps occupy yourself with your sketch book."

It sounded more like an instruction than a suggestion.

And she resented being told what to do.

For the briefest of moments she wondered whether she would go to the kennel deck and exercise Muffin.

Then she realised that what she really wanted was to see Lord Castleton again.

*

Over the next few days, as the ship sailed nearer and nearer to Malta, Justina struggled with her letter to her parents.

Each day, as she spent more time with Sir Thomas, she was made more and more aware of his autocratic nature.

If she suggested they might play a game of deck quoits with the Arbuthnot girls and the Subalterns, he would tell her he wanted to rehearse the songs he was to sing in the concert.

If, however, she proposed that they rehearse together, he declared that he was committed to playing whist.

Every night either Sir Thomas dined at the Arbuthnot table or they dined at his.

The Arbuthnots would listen to his tales of Bombay with seeming fascination. Justina soon tired of stories that always featured Sir Thomas in some heroic light or demeaned some poor Indian.

At first, Justina had produced questions, eager to understand more of the intriguing land that was India. In the early days of their relationship, Sir Thomas had responded in detail.

Now he grew impatient with her thirst for knowledge and expected her to produce the sort of admiring comments that Faith and Charity were always making.

Dancing with her after dinner one night, he once again made the suggestion that they went outside.

"Everyone is fascinated with the moon," he said,

holding her closely. "It is almost full and painting a silver path upon the sea."

It sounded wonderful and Justina allowed Sir Thomas to take her onto the deck.

The sight was indeed beautiful, the sky a velvety darkness, the moon hanging low in the sky, spreading a silken veil of light over ship and sea, its reflection luminous on the water.

There were other passengers on deck, appreciating the lovely scene, but Sir Thomas soon guided her into one of the many shadowy areas.

There he pulled Justina into his arms and pressed a passionate kiss onto her. Taken by surprise, she could not object, but as his mouth ground into hers she started to struggle.

She felt none of the rapture she had always assumed came when you were kissed by an attractive man – rather a fierce repulsion filled her.

Her attempts to free herself only seemed to excite him further.

Eventually he raised his head, but continued to hold her hard against him.

"No, my dear little Justina," he gurgled, his voice slurred. "You cannot refuse me. I am your fiancé and I have the right to expect a goodnight kiss from you."

His eyelids were half closed, his mouth full and sensual.

Hopelessness coursed through her.

Is this what love was about? How was she to cope with his demands?

A cry suddenly rent the night air. It was a cry full of horror.

People came running onto the deck to see what was the

matter.

Sir Thomas had no option but to release Justina and she found herself running with the others.

A woman was standing in a quiet corner towards the stern of the ship.

"It was Charlie," she kept crying. "My Charlie. He was there, I swear it, *he was there*."

Patience Wright came up, followed by her husband.

"My dear Mrs. Partridge, there is no one there. You are distressed. Come with me, we will find the Major."

She put her arm round the woman.

Justina had noticed Mrs. Partridge after the ship had sailed from Gibraltar. Slender and very pale, she carried an air of tragedy around with her. She was accompanied by her husband, a military man of quiet dignity. He looked after her with great care but said very little. Now he hurried up.

A moment later his wife was weeping in his arms.

"Poor woman," said someone standing beside Justina. "She will never get over the loss of her son. They came over from India to visit his grave. Died in school of a fever. They hadn't seen him since he left Calcutta two years ago."

There was a general murmur of distress as the passengers started to disperse.

Sir Thomas took hold of Justina's elbow, but she withdrew her arm.

"I am very tired, I think I will retire now. Why don't you enjoy a cigar?"

In her cabin she found the beginnings of the letter she was trying to write to her parents.

She read through the few lines that she had managed, but in her ears she heard the distress in the woman's voice as she described seeing the ghost of her son.

How awful to have lost your beloved child. And how

awful not to have seen him for two years! Was that what happened to children you bore in India? Would she bear children to Sir Thomas, pour her love and her life into them and then have her whole reason for living snatched away?

The very idea was too much and Justina dissolved into tears.

In his cabin next door, Lord Castleton was working through yet more papers.

He was in his shirt sleeves, the porthole beside him wide open. The night air held a softness that demonstrated they were well into the Mediterranean's warmth.

He sighed. Heat enervated the mind and made it more difficult to concentrate.

But he knew that it was not the Mediterranean air that prevented him taking in the subtleties of the papers he was trying to read.

It was the picture that Justina had made that evening, dressed in a white lace dress that set off her extraordinary hair. He had hoped to have finished his meal before she arrived but the service was slow that night.

Sir Thomas had welcomed the Arbuthnots to his table and the simpering girls had settled themselves before Justina entered the Saloon.

He found he was gazing at her like any lovesick youth.

He came to with a start, but not before Justina's wide grey eyes had gazed into his for a heart-stopping moment.

He would have raised his glass to her, but out of the corner of his eye he saw Sir Thomas take in the glance and his face darken.

When next he glanced towards Watson's table, Justina was seated, her head bowed over her menu.

Lord Castleton had a sudden vision of her eyes full of tears.

He was furious with himself that he was handling the situation that had arisen between her, Watson and himself so badly.

He was known as a diplomat, a man who managed every circumstance with debonair charm or quiet tact, whatever was required.

Yet now he was blundering about in a way that failed to solve the central problem and merely increased Justina's embarrassment.

Reaching to ring for the Steward to bring him a large brandy, he stayed his hand and listened.

Was that what he thought it was?

After a moment he was certain. But did the weeping come from the cabin on his right or his left?

Rising in one fluid movement, he strode out of his cabin and stood outside Justina's door.

Any remaining doubt was removed from his mind.

He raised his hand and knocked.

The weeping stopped but no one answered.

Squaring his shoulders, he gave another knock and opened the door.

Justina sat at a similar table to his with a piece of paper in front of her. It looked as if she had been writing, but the paper was blotched with her tears.

She raised her eyes to his in total surprise.

"My Lord, what – what can I do for you?"

He came in and sat down on a corner of the table, leaving the door half open.

"Justina, I cannot hear you in distress without offering you my help in whatever situation is causing you such unhappiness."

She gulped.

"My Lord, I am not in distress. At least – " she glanced down at the tear-strewn letter. "It is only – only that I am writing to my parents and, all at once, I felt very, very homesick."

She would not meet his eyes but fiddled with her pen.

"Is that really *all* that is the matter?"

She said nothing and he felt he had to reinforce his role as her father's friend.

"I know Lord Mansell would want me to offer my help if his daughter was in any trouble."

At that remark she flared up.

"I am not in trouble, my Lord. I am very happy. Sir Thomas is a good man and I am indeed fortunate that he wishes to marry me. That is why I am writing to my parents."

Lord Castleton felt helpless.

There was nothing he actually knew for certain against Watson.

All that Ariadne had told him had been in confidence. To breathe a word of any of it would reflect upon her cousin, the girl in the affair. And, perhaps, just perhaps, there had been some misunderstanding over what had happened.

He knew Ariadne had disapproved of Watson, well, he had never liked the man himself, but had she, perhaps, exaggerated the situation in some way?

And he had no proof that Watson was in financial difficulties.

"In that case, I will leave you," he said slowly.

Justina continued to look at him with bright eyes, her colour heightened, her hands tightly clasped in her lap.

He wanted to gather her in his arms and tell her everything would be all right and he would make sure she never had any reason to cry ever again.

Instead, he rose.

"Please, though, remember that I am only in the next cabin. If ever you are in need, you have only to call out."

"I shall not need you, my Lord," she replied steadily. "But you are very kind. My father will be most appreciative."

She looked at the half-open cabin door and for the first time betrayed nervousness.

"I would be grateful if you could leave me now."

Immediately he understood. If Mrs. Arbuthnot or, perish the thought, Watson, came by, he would have placed her in a most difficult position.

"Of course," he agreed and departed, moving back to his own cabin as quickly as he could.

How much of what she had said could he trust? Was he only wishing her engagement to Sir Thomas at an end because he wanted to woo her himself? At their first meeting he had accused her of anthropomorphism, of assuming that Muffin could feel what she felt. Was he now guilty of much the same transference of thought?

He rang the bell and ordered his brandy.

Left alone, Justina discarded her latest effort at writing to her parents, drew out a clean piece of paper and, without thought, wrote quickly and succinctly.

"Dearest Mama and Papa,

I have met among the passengers on this ship, Sir Thomas Watson. He is writing to you by the same mail from Malta, asking for my hand in marriage. He has met Papa and I hope you will able to grant his request. I am very happy to have attracted the attentions of someone who will be such a suitable husband.

With much love, your darling daughter,

Justina."

Without reading it through, she placed it in an envelope, sealed it and wrote the address.

At long last she felt able to undress.

As she removed the white lace dress, she realised for the first time the hazards of having written her letter whilst wearing it. Suppose the ship had pitched unexpectedly and she had spilt ink on it!

Even that horrid thought, however, could not drive away the anguish she had felt at Lord Castleton's unexpected arrival in her cabin.

He had been so kind!

She had wanted to throw herself into his arms and beg him to sort out the awful mess she was in. Instead all she could think was that her love for him was hopeless and how embarrassing he would find it if she did.

Now she crept into her bed, drew up the covers and, as silently as she was able, wept herself to sleep.

*

By the time Justina woke the next morning, they had docked in Valletta harbour. Once again there was all the bustle and cries of a foreign port.

Justina had thought of going ashore to find a present for her brother. They were to be in port for nine hours, plenty of time to find a shop.

She was hoping that, by the time she was ready to leave the ship, Sir Thomas would have gone ashore. She had already told the Arbuthnot girls that she was not interested in seeing Valletta.

If only, she thought, she could have a day by herself, untroubled by thoughts of the future and maybe she would be able to act as she should towards Sir Thomas.

A quick trip to some shops, maybe a little look into the Cathedral and then back to sit in the sun and do some sketching.

She went and put on a broad hat to shade her face from the sun that was growing stronger before hastening towards the gangway.

"Ah, my Justina," said Sir Thomas, suddenly appearing by her side. "I was coming to look for you. The Misses Arbuthnot told me you were not going ashore, but I can see that you are indeed planning to visit Valletta. Now we can go together."

"No, Sir Thomas." Justina smiled up at him, immediately changing her plans and trying to be at her most pleasant. "It is very kind of you to think of accompanying me, but I was only going to walk around the Promenade Deck. Then I have set aside the rest of the day for sketching."

"Nonsense. You cannot miss the opportunity of visiting this ancient town. It is historic, you know."

"What is its claim to fame?"

Justina thought if only she could keep him talking, one of the men friends he had made on the ship would come by and suggest a visit to the smoking room.

"I don't bother myself with history." His eyes gleamed suddenly. "But I always take the prettiest girl on the ship to visit the Cathedral. You can see that I cannot miss taking you."

Almost Justina wavered. He seemed to be in such a pleasant mood.

"Maybe later?"

His eyes narrowed.

"You are not going to prove a difficult wife, I hope, Justina? I would counsel you to be careful how you toy with me."

He gripped her arm, in exactly the same place where he had inflicted a bruise previously and ignored her yelp of pain.

"You must learn that when I say something I mean it. When I ask you to come ashore with me, I mean now, not later, not this afternoon, not next voyage, but *now*."

He forced her to accompany him towards the gangway. Justina stumbled in her effort to keep up with him. She looked around to see if there was anyone who could divert Sir Thomas from his course of action. But most of the passengers had already gone ashore and there was no one to witness the way he was abusing her.

Her sense of duty to the man she had allowed herself to become engaged to dictated that she followed him down the gangway.

The Cathedral was huge and dark.

"Is that not magnificent?" Sir Thomas proclaimed proudly as they entered. "Are you not impressed?"

Justina looked at the banners that decorated each of a large number of bays on either side of the Church.

"What do they mean?" she asked.

"No idea but the effect is grand."

"Each bay is dedicated to one of the countries of the Knights that made up the Order of St John," said a voice behind them.

Sir Thomas cursed as he swung round to confront Lord Castleton.

"Have we asked you to accompany us around?" he snarled.

"I apologise," said Lord Castleton, seeming not a whit disturbed by his reception. "I hoped to increase your pleasure of this noble edifice by some information on the dedication that lies behind its erection."

Justina wanted above all for Lord Castleton to take them around. She was sure he could tell them the history not only of the Church, but also of Malta itself and the Order of St John. She knew, though, that this was a hopeless wish.

"I will thank you to keep your information to yourself," snapped Sir Thomas, aggression suffusing his voice and stance. "Come, Justina, we have seen enough."

He gripped Justina's upper arm and walked her out of the cool, dark nave and into the bright sunlight.

She was afraid to say anything lest she provoke him further.

"We shall return to the ship. After all, didn't you say that you wished to sketch a view of Valletta?" said Sir Thomas.

Justina gave a last glance to the impressive outline of the Cathedral of St John and looked at the Spanish-influenced architecture that lay all around them.

"It all looks most interesting and it is pleasant to be on stable land after the ship, though it is strange how it seems to move as though one was still at sea."

"When you are a more seasoned traveller, you will realise it is a hazard to be encountered every time you have been sailing," Sir Thomas replied in a more pleasant tone.

They came to a pleasant piazza where there were tables and chairs in the sun and Justina recognised some fellow passengers enjoying a refreshing drink.

"Perhaps," she murmured, thinking how pleasant it would be to join them. "We could sit down and you could tell me more about your travels?"

For a moment she thought he would agree and then a disfiguring redness flushed his face.

"You hope Castleton will join us, don't you? Maybe you have already arranged such a meeting?"

Justina stopped walking and looked directly at him.

"I do not arrange clandestine assignations, Sir Thomas, with Lord Castleton or anyone else. If our relationship is to be a success, you must accept that I am, above all things, honest."

For the first time since Justina had met him, Sir Thomas appeared to be at a loss. But only for a moment.

"Why, of course you are, my dear. It is not only for your beauty that I have fallen so quickly and so irrevocably in love with you. Come, I believe you, but I wish to return to the ship where we can lunch quietly and you may be able to sketch in peace."

Feeling unexpectedly reassured by his attitude, Justina was happy to accompany him.

Lord Castleton watched Justina and Sir Thomas leave the Cathedral. He was incensed beyond measure at the man's rudeness.

Justina was never going to happy with such a husband.

Next he recognised that he had to do everything he could to release her from an engagement that promised nothing but unhappiness. Not just because he was in love with her, but because he had to rescue her from what would be a lifetime of regret.

How, though, was he to do this, he wondered, regarding a dark oil painting of the Madonna and child.

As he looked without seeing at the Virgin's sad face, he realised that in a battle with Thomas Watson, he had a powerful weapon.

Several times the man had come close to losing control when he had appeared on the scene.

Watson was jealous. The fact that he had nothing to be jealous about did not matter.

Of course, he thought, it was quite obvious what he should do.

He made his way down the nave of the Cathedral.

He had to start a campaign and he knew exactly what his first move should be.

CHAPTER EIGHT

Justina spent a peaceful afternoon sketching Valletta from the upper deck.

Soon after she began her sketch, there was a flurry of activity as a woman dressed in the height of fashion arrived at the quayside accompanied by a large amount of luggage.

Justina admired the woman's severely tailored and immaculate cream linen skirt and jacket, trimmed with a great deal of dark brown braid. A mass of dark brown hair was arranged into waves gathered into a complicated knot at the back of her head and topped with a dashing small pill-box hat decorated with feathers.

This was a lady of considerable style.

Justina returned to her sketching.

That evening, with the ship once again at sea, its engines throbbing as it thrust through the calm waters towards the Suez Canal, Justina was surprised to see that the Arbuthnot table had been laid for six.

"Is it Tony or Bertie who is joining us?" she asked Charity. The two Arbuthnot girls were spending considerable time with the young Subalterns.

"Neither," said Charity with a triumphant smile. "Faith has asked Lord Castleton to dine with us."

"And he has agreed?"

"Why should you be so surprised?" Faith smirked at her. "You are not the only girl who can attract eligible men."

"Darling Faith is *so* pretty," oozed Mrs. Arbuthnot. "One cannot wonder at Lord Castleton being captivated by her. When he approached her coming back from Valletta, I knew he had only been waiting for the right moment. After all, who can resist her charms?

"Ah, Sir Thomas," she said as Sir Thomas came up to the table. "How pleasant to see you. You have, I trust, enjoyed your sojourn in Valletta? And I know you will be delighted to hear that Lord Castleton is to join our happy little table this evening."

Caught in the act of greeting Justina, Sir Thomas's body became rigid, his face an unreadable mask.

"You don't say!"

"Evening, Watson," called Lord Castleton, approaching the table at that moment. "Mrs. Arbuthnot was kind enough to invite me to join her little party and I thought it unfair that you should have four of the loveliest young ladies on the ship all to yourself."

Justina could hardly believe it. The only time she had seen Lord Castleton at all informal had been exercising the dogs. She remembered how cold he had been when Faith had walked Muffin at the same time as he had Breck.

She could have sworn that he would have absolutely no interest in either of the Arbuthnot sisters.

Yet here he was at their table.

Sir Thomas sat down, his eyes narrowed suspiciously, but was unable to think of anything to say.

Dinner proceeded with Lord Castleton as the leading light of the party. He was witty and courteous, drawing out Faith and Charity and listening without a hint of boredom to Mrs. Arbuthnot's interminable stories about life on the Afghan border.

The one person Lord Castleton did not show any interest in was Justina. At first she was relieved as she had no desire to have Sir Thomas reacting badly should she be singled out for attention.

After a while, however, as her pulse stopped racing and her breathing returned to normal, she began to resent the lack of attention. She realised she had grown used to the feeling that she was someone special to Lord Castleton, even if only as a sort of niece.

Then Lord Castleton started addressing remarks to Sir Thomas, quizzing him in the nicest possible way on his business in Bombay.

All he received were evasions and remarks such as,

"Not much fun for the ladies, discussing business, Castleton, don't you know?"

Gone were his confident stories and teasing of Mrs. Arbuthnot, he sat glowering until dessert.

Then, suddenly, he said,

"Brought Ariadne out to India, did you, Castleton? What did she think of all the native wallahs?"

Justina saw something flash in Lord Castleton's eyes. For a moment she thought he would retreat into the reserved manner he had shown so often.

He smiled easily and replied,

"Alas, my dear wife died before she could come out. I regret very much that I had not arranged a trip earlier. She expressed great interest in India and the complexity of its peoples and religions."

There was a short silence at the table. Justina tried to think of something to say that would ease the conversation into a different area without sounding obvious.

Instead Mrs. Russell stopped at their table on her way out of the Saloon. Looking straight at Justina, she said,

"Thank you so much, Miss Mansell, for agreeing to perform a duet with Lord Castleton at our little concert the night before we reach the Suez Canal. Remember, my dears, rehearsal tomorrow afternoon."

She swept on, followed by the Colonel.

"Justina, you have told me nothing of a duet," Sir Thomas queried in a dangerously quiet voice.

She looked at him in complete astonishment.

"I knew nothing about it."

"Is this your doing, Castleton?"

Lord Castleton gave him a happy smile.

"I am sorry, I should have asked Justina first, but since we had played it together before we reached Gibraltar, I knew it would be a complete success and Mrs. Russell mentioned to me that they were short of suitable numbers."

Justina thought Sir Thomas was going to explode.

"If it will help Mrs. Russell's Entertainment's Committee," she said hastily, "I am very happy to assist in any way I can."

"I would have thought," brayed Sir Thomas in a loud voice that had people looking at their table. "I would have thought," he repeated, "that accompanying *me* would have been enough for Justina. I think it is very selfish of you, Castleton, not to find another pianist to show off with."

"Tut tut," Mrs. Arbuthnot intervened. "Sir Thomas, I am sure Lord Castleton is not being selfish. I do so admire men prepared, as you are, Sir Thomas, to put themselves out to entertain us. I am so looking forward to our concert."

At the end of the meal Lord Castleton suggested that they moved to the Lounge, where there was dancing.

Sir Thomas took a firm grasp of Justina's arm and insisted on taking her onto the floor as soon as they arrived.

"I cannot believe that you have been so reckless as to

agree to play with Castleton and I forbid you to do so."

Justina looked up at him with wide eyes.

"But won't Mrs. Russell wonder why you should object to the item? Will it not give rise to just the sort of speculation I assume you are anxious to avoid?"

She was determined to perform the duet.

"I cannot understand why you should object," she continued. "Lord Castleton is a friend of my father and it will almost be like playing with him, which I am sure we should have done had dearest Papa been with us on the ship."

She saw Lord Castleton circling the floor with Mrs. Arbuthnot and wondered if he would ask her to dance.

Should she accept his invitation if he did?

Then Lord Castleton asked first Faith and next Charity to take the floor.

Finally he came to her. But before he could speak, Sir Thomas said very firmly.

"I thought you said you had a headache, Justina, and wished to retire."

"How very unfortunate," sympathised Lord Castleton. "I hope your headache will soon go, I want both of us to be at our best for tomorrow's rehearsal."

It was such a lovely moment to look forward to, Justina was almost happy to allow Sir Thomas to escort her back to her cabin.

As they reached her door, she said,

"You are quite right about my headache, Sir Thomas, I think I am very tired after our exploration of Valletta today. Thank you for our dance."

She turned the key in the lock and waited until she heard his footsteps fade away along the corridor. She sank onto her bed wondering if she would ever be able to learn how to handle him.

The rehearsal went badly. Sir Thomas kept stopping his songs and complaining that she needed to put more emotion into her accompaniment.

"I do not want to outshine your singing," she said as mildly as she could manage after the third time he had asked her for greater emphasis in her phrasing.

He glared at her.

"I appreciate your concern, but I do not think you need worry too much."

At that moment Lord Castleton entered the Lounge.

He sat down in a chair near to the piano and appeared to take a frank and enthusiastic interest in the proceedings.

Sir Thomas started to sing more and more quickly and Justina had to struggle to keep up with him.

At the end of the song, he turned to her and her heart quailed at the look on his face.

"I expect you to keep better time tonight," he growled in a furious undertone. "Come with me now."

Justina continued to sit at the piano.

"I need to rehearse with Lord Castleton," she told him calmly. "Mrs. Russell and the Committee expect it."

At that moment Mrs. Russell spoke up,

"Lord Castleton, whilst Miss Mansell is at the piano, would you be so good as to join her so you can run through your piece?" She gave a pleasant smile. "I am sure, Sir Thomas, you will come over quite beautifully this evening."

"You are too kind, Mrs. Russell," Sir Thomas said as Lord Castleton moved to sit beside Justina.

Justina found her heart beating at an almost unbearable rate.

Then Lord Castleton smiled at her.

"Pretend we are all alone. We are just going to enjoy ourselves."

It was the smile rather than the words that quietened Justina's racing heart. She found the presence of everyone else in the Lounge, including Sir Thomas, fading away.

She smiled back at Lord Castleton and raised her hands. He gave a slight nod and they began.

As the light and sparkling music unfolded, its melodies twisting and soaring, Justina was transported into a world where nothing else existed.

She felt herself one with the man sitting beside her, their hands bound together in the music, instinctively knowing that they shared an identical interpretation.

It was not a case of one leading and the other following, they played in perfect harmony.

As the last notes faded away, Justina sat completely still and looked out beyond the piano through the wide windows of the Lounge to the blue of the Mediterranean that seemed to promise both untold depths and scintillating lights.

If only that light could illuminate her life, she thought.

"Thank you," Lord Castleton said quietly. "That was perfect."

There was spontaneous applause from the other performers in the Lounge.

"Until tonight," said Lord Castleton, rising from the piano stool.

At the end of the rehearsal, Mrs. Russell thanked all the participants.

"I wish you all luck and I am certain you will acquit yourselves well. May I emphasise that no one is to perform an encore, otherwise we shall be there until after midnight."

People began to drift away, talking enthusiastically.

Justina was very conscious of Lord Castleton standing beside her.

Then Sir Thomas came up.

"I think you promised me a walk round the deck," he said imperiously to Justina. "Then you will need to rest before the exertions of this evening."

Justina allowed herself to be led out of the Lounge and forced herself not to look back at Lord Castleton.

Walking round the deck with Sir Thomas, she listened to a stream of instructions on when her accompaniment should add emphasis to his phrasing.

"What you have to understand," he said at one point, "is that the song is telling a story. The singer really wants Maud to come into the garden." He paused for a moment. "I imagine that you are the girl I am singing to and that is why I am so anxious to be as persuasive as I can."

Justina was so taken aback at this she was unable to respond.

"You are the girl to whom I have given my heart and the idea that you might not feel the same way about me is insupportable."

He walked quickly past two passengers leaning over the railing, deep in conversation and repeated,

"Insupportable. If, on occasion, I may seem a little abrupt, that is why."

Justina struggled to find something to say.

"Sir Thomas – " she started.

"Why do you always address me by my title? Eh? Why cannot you say, Thomas?"

"Because you have never said that is what you would like," Justina fired back at him, now completely bewildered by the turn in his conversation.

"Do I have to tell you everything?" Sir Thomas was

winding himself up now. "I hope you are not going to be one of those wives who expects their husband to think for them."

They had reached the stern of the ship. No one was around them. Justina stopped and turned to face Sir Thomas.

"I often find it difficult to know how to respond to you," she said slowly. "I am not one of those girls who needs to be told, I have my own ideas, but I have found in our relationship that too often you do not like either what I say or what I do."

She stood with beating heart. Would this prompt him to state that perhaps it might be best if they dissolved the understanding between them? And if he did, what were her parents going to say?

They would be so pleased to receive the letters that said she had contracted such a good match and were they then to be doomed to disappointment by her next letter saying that she was no longer engaged?

"What an extraordinary thing to say, Justina. I am always delighted at your unexpected opinions and I find your views refreshing. The only time – " his voice hardened and acquired a steely overtone.

"The only time I have to take issue with you is when you insult me by disobeying a reasonable request or laying yourself open to the world's condemnation by, for instance, encouraging the attentions of a mountebank such as Lord Castleton. No, don't say anything," he held up a hand as Justina opened her mouth to defend herself.

"I am not at all happy about your playing this ridiculous duet with Castleton, but there is nothing I can do about it, not without exposing you in a way that would damage your reputation and that would never be my intention."

He was breathing hard now and white patches appeared on either side of his nostrils.

131

Justina had to believe that he really did have her best interests at heart.

"I am glad to hear that, Sir – I mean, Thomas. I am sorry you do not like my duet with Lord Castleton," she continued earnestly. "I can assure you there is nothing in my friendship with him to which you can take exception."

She held herself very upright and looked him straight in the eye.

He said nothing but his colour heightened.

*

That evening Dorcas came to Justina's cabin.

"I am much better," she announced. "I can help to dress you."

She looked very pale and had lost weight.

"Are you sure you are better?" asked Justina doubtfully. "You do not look at all strong. I have managed so far on my own, I am sure another night will not matter."

"I *am* better," Dorcas repeated with emphasis. "Now that the ship no longer moves in that dreadful way, I shall be fine."

Justina had to admit that Dorcas did a much better job on her hair than she could achieve herself. Somehow she managed to tame its wild curls and arrange it in attractive waves drawn up behind and culminating in a Grecian knot.

"Which dress will you wear?" asked Dorcas, examining the small number of gowns Justina had brought up from the baggage hold. "If you are playing in this concert, I think the grey would be best – it has authority!"

"Yes, Dorcas, I think you are right."

All through dinner, Justina suffered terrible nerves. She was convinced that her fingers would stumble over the keys, that she would ruin Sir Thomas's songs and leave Lord Castleton playing all alone in the duet.

Then copies of the programme for the evening's entertainment arrived.

"Good Heavens," exclaimed Charity. "You are the final item, Justina."

"With me?" enquired Sir Thomas eagerly.

"No. You are the third item. It is Justina's duet with Lord Castleton that ends the concert."

For a moment Justina thought that Sir Thomas would approach Mrs. Russell to demand that the programme be altered.

"They need you to get everyone enjoying the concert," she told him.

He would have said something but Faith rose.

"Come on, we have to assemble in the Lounge," she said. "Remember that Mrs. Russell said none of us was to be late."

"I have missed my brandy," Sir Thomas complained. "My vocal chords will not perform well without one."

He went and found a Steward.

"Are you nervous?" Lord Castleton asked Justina.

She nodded, unable to speak.

"There is no need, you will be perfect."

Justina felt even more nervous.

Sir Thomas returned, followed by a Steward with a glass of brandy. But by then Lord Castleton was in conversation with the conjuror.

All too soon the Lounge doors were opened and the passengers poured in, talking excitedly.

Justina sat on a chair at the side, twisting her hands in her lap.

Looking up at one point, she saw Lord Castleton smile at her and somehow he made her feel a tiny bit better.

The concert opened with a girl singing to her own accompaniment, next there was a recitation and then it was Sir Thomas's turn.

Justina sat at the piano and arranged the music. Sir Thomas stood in its curve as he knew the songs by heart.

It was hard work accompanying him, because Sir Thomas lengthened and shortened phrases as he judged the most effective.

Still at the end he received hearty applause. He bowed again and again and said he would respond to the appreciation with an encore. Justina caught a glimpse of Mrs. Russell's shocked face before Sir Thomas turned over the pages to a song he had sung only once before.

The applause at the end was much less than earlier and Justina knew Sir Thomas would blame her.

Justina felt a little better.

All too soon it was time for the last item on the programme.

Justina walked forward with Lord Castleton to the piano and they arranged themselves on the seat.

"You look wonderful," he whispered. "And you played superbly both in the Chopin and when you accompanied Sir Thomas."

She felt heartened.

Once again she lost herself in the wonder of playing with Lord Castleton. It was so different from accompanying Sir Thomas, where she had so little contact with his interpretation of the music.

The applause at the end was tumultuous.

Justina stood beside Lord Castleton and shyly bowed in response.

Without thinking, Justina sank into a little curtsy and

smiled up at him. Then she walked away and joined Sir Thomas.

"Did you think it went well?" she asked him, a note of supplication in her voice.

"You were very good," he mumbled.

Many people congratulated both Justina and Sir Thomas and he ordered a bottle of champagne to celebrate.

Faith and Charity came over with their mother and the two Subalterns.

Lord Castleton had moved over to the other side of the Lounge and was talking to the fashionable lady who had come aboard at Malta. He appeared to be enjoying the conversation.

"I gather her name is Mrs. Bloxham," Mrs. Arbuthnot confided. "I think she is a widow. Probably looking for another husband. Well, with a name like Bloxham, why wouldn't she? I know I would if I was saddled in that way."

Justina felt very tired.

It had been an exhausting day.

She looked around. Sir Thomas was in conversation with one of his cronies.

It seemed a perfect opportunity to slip away and be spared the difficult business of preventing him entering her cabin to kiss her goodnight.

With a sigh of thankfulness, she walked to her cabin, grateful that she had told Dorcas not to wait up for her.

She slipped through the door and locked it behind her.

Next she discovered that she was not alone.

Someone else was in her cabin.

CHAPTER NINE

Justina opened her mouth to scream.

Then she realised that her intruder was a small boy, a very scared small boy.

He was dressed in stained and torn grey flannel trousers and a shirt that had once been white and now was indescribably dirty. The sleeves were rolled up, buttons were missing and if he had ever worn a tie, it had disappeared.

"Who are you and what are you doing in my cabin?" Justina demanded.

"Please, miss, my name is Harry Nicholls and I'm very hungry."

He did indeed look half-starved.

His eyes were an intense dark blue and huge in his small face. This was not someone she need be frightened of.

"Where have you appeared from?"

He glanced over her shoulder at the porthole.

"I've – I've been living in one of the lifeboats."

"One of the lifeboats?" Justina repeated, horror-struck. "You mean, you are a stowaway?"

Harry nodded.

"But why?" Justina could not imagine how the small boy had found his way onto the ship.

His eyes filled with tears.

"I want to go home," he answered and his voice wobbled.

"Where is home?" Justina asked gently.

"Bombay, miss. That's where Mama and Papa live and my two little sisters and – that's where I want to go."

"But – " Justina could not understand why, if that was the case, young Harry was not with them.

"They sent me to England, miss, to school. All children go to school in England when they are old enough, Papa said. And – and he said I was old enough and it would be fine. Only it wasn't – "

Tears poured down his face.

"They beat me at school and the other boys are awful. They hate me because I can't play rugger and I like reading poetry. And I spent the summer holidays with Aunt Martha and she, well, I think she hates boys. She doesn't let me have any friends and I'm not allowed to make a noise or do anything that she says 'gets in the way'.

"She never kisses me or tells me I'm a good boy. She's always saying she's taken me in as a duty!" he ended on a wail. "I want Mama and Papa and Milly and Agatha – and my Ayah."

Justina hugged him hard and did not care if his tears stained her gown.

"So you thought if you jumped on this ship, you would get back to India?"

He nodded and dug his fists into his eyes to stop his tears.

"There was a boy joined the school late. His parents brought him. I heard one of the Masters ask them if they were returning on the new ship and they said, no, it was leaving the next day and they had business or something in London. So then I thought I would hide away on it."

The magnitude of what he had done astounded Justina.

"How did you know where to find the docks?"

"When Papa and I came last spring," again there was an unhappy wobble in his voice. "We went from the boat to the school by train. I knew where the station was."

"Did you have money for the ticket?"

Harry shook his head.

"There was a family with lots of children going onto the platform, so I just went along with them. And when we got to the docks, I found another family and followed them onto the ship. It was easy!"

"And how did you find a lifeboat?"

"When we came over on the ship – it was much smaller than this one – Papa told me all about lifeboats, how they had what he called 'iron rations', in case everybody had to abandon ship. So I thought I'd be able to live in one and I had all the chocolate from my tuck box. But that soon went and I could only find dry biscuits in the boat and tins of things that I couldn't open."

Justina remembered the passengers who had complained that someone had taken fruit from their cabin.

"So you started to climb into people's cabins to find food? You came into mine."

Harry looked shamefaced.

Justina could not understand how he had kept going for so long. No wonder he looked so rough.

"My lifeboat is just outside your window, miss, and I'd seen you often and you looked friendly, so I hoped – well, I hoped you could help me, miss."

"Of course I will," Justina promised, wondering exactly what she could do.

Suddenly there came a loud knocking at the door.

"Justina, let me in. I want to say goodnight to you."

It was Sir Thomas.

Harry looked startled and apprehensive.

Justina put a finger to her lips. Then she called,

"I am going to bed, Sir Thomas. I will see you in the morning."

"You've got someone in there, I know you have, I heard you talking to him. It's Castleton and I won't have it, *open the door*."

His voice was low, urgent and aggressive.

"There isn't any man in here," Justina protested.

She glanced around the cabin then motioned to Harry to get under the bed.

He understood immediately and in a moment had wriggled himself out of sight.

Justina, pretending the pause had been necessary so she could refasten the buttons on the back of her dress, opened the door a little.

"You are making a great mistake," she told Sir Thomas.

At that moment Lord Castleton came along the corridor towards his cabin.

"Good evening," he said pleasantly. "The concert went well, didn't it?" He unlocked his door. "See you in the morning," he added as he went inside.

"See?" hissed Justina at Sir Thomas. "See how ill-founded all your suspicions are. She flung open the door for a brief moment. "Nobody is here and certainly not Lord Castleton."

She immediately tried to close the door again, but Sir Thomas stuck a foot in.

"I insist on my goodnight kiss," he pressed in a different tone.

Justina realised with a sinking heart that he had drunk several brandies since the end of the concert.

Then along the corridor came Mrs. Bloxham, her bosom prominently displayed by her low-cut green silk gown.

"Sir Thomas," she exclaimed in a low voice that seemed to throb. "You are just the man I need."

His attention immediately switched away from Justina.

"Indeed, madam? What can I do to help?"

"But I do not wish to intrude," Mrs. Bloxham purred suggestively. "It's only," she continued without a pause, "it's only that this ship is so large and the corridors so confusing. I cannot find my cabin – isn't that ridiculous?"

She gave a rich little laugh.

Justina seized on the interruption.

"Sir Thomas will help you, madam. Until tomorrow morning, Sir Thomas, I think we shall be in Port Said then."

Justina closed the door and lay against it, listening.

Their voices faded along the corridor.

"Can I come out?" whispered Harry.

"Yes, of course, let me help you."

Justina pulled the boy from underneath the bed.

She wondered exactly how to help him. Food was an obvious necessity, but she could not force him to return to his lifeboat and what was the alternative?

He stared back at her, his big eyes apprehensive.

She came to a decision.

"Stay here," she ordered. "I will be back in a moment."

She whisked herself out of the cabin and knocked on Lord Castleton's door.

He opened it and looked at her with surprise and concern.

"Miss Mansell, is anything wrong?"

"Please, can you come with me," she entreated. "I don't know who else to ask."

Just the sight of him, tall, kindly and authoritative, made her completely confident that he would find a solution to Harry's problem.

He raised an eyebrow but murmured helpfully,

"Of course, anything I can do," and followed her back into her cabin.

As Justina watched with eager anticipation, Lord Castleton took in Harry and his filthy clothes and it seemed as if he understood everything in a glance.

"So, this is the ghost who caused so much upset the other day," he observed. "You had better give me the full story."

Lord Castleton leant against the side of the cabin and Justina sat beside Harry on the bed as the boy once again explained how he had come to be on the ship.

As he faltered to the end of his account, Lord Castleton said,

"Well, the first thing is to get some food inside you."

He opened the door of the cabin – and came face to face with Sir Thomas.

"I knew it," Sir Thomas cried. "I knew you were canoodling with my fiancée."

Lord Castleton looked at him coldly.

"Don't make more of a fool of yourself than you can help, Watson."

He opened the door fully and revealed Harry.

"As you can see, we have a stowaway problem here.

Miss Mansell has very properly called on me to help solve it."

Sir Thomas looked as though he could hardly believe the evidence of his eyes.

"Send for the Captain," he said. "The boy should be confined to quarters then put ashore at Port Said."

"No!" cried out Harry. "I am going to Bombay."

"Quarters, what do you mean by quarters? He's been living in a lifeboat!" Justina burst out. "I am going to find a Steward and make sure he gets some food."

She had never felt less in sympathy with her fiancé. Whereas Lord Castleton treated Harry as someone in need of help, Sir Thomas saw him as a nuisance to be disposed of.

She could hardly bear to think of what that poor boy had suffered. She wanted to gather him into her arms and keep him safe from the harsh world.

Justina did not know what Lord Castleton would do, but she had complete faith in his ability to sort the situation out and ensure Harry reached Bombay.

As she sought out a Steward and ordered whatever food could be quickly assembled, she thrust the problem of Sir Thomas to the back of her mind.

When she returned to the cabin, she found Lord Castleton had got Harry washed and into what she assumed was one of his shirts, which hung on the boy rather like a night shirt, his bare feet peeking out of the bottom, small neck.

"Sartorially speaking," Lord Castleton said, "I don't think any tailor would approve, but it's better than what you've had to live in for the past ten days, eh?"

Harry grinned at him.

"It's very kind of you, sir."

She looked around the cabin. It only contained the

three of them.

"What has happened to Sir Thomas?" she asked.

"Ah," said Lord Castleton. "I am afraid I may have frightened him away.

"Frightened?" Justina found this hard to believe.

"I told him you would be so grateful if he took on responsibility for Harry, which would probably mean paying his fare to Bombay and equipping him with a new wardrobe in Port Said."

"No?"

"Oh, but yes!" he said in amusement. "He immediately claimed that you would think he had lost his head if he did anything of the sort and discovered that he had arranged to meet someone in the Smoking Lounge."

"He looked jolly cross," contributed Harry. "I didn't like him at all, sir."

"Did not your Papa tell you it is very rude to make personal comments, especially about someone you have only just met?" scolded him Justina severely.

Harry hung his head.

"I'm sorry, miss," he said. "Only he wasn't very nice to me, not like you and – and, sir here."

"This is Lord Castleton," Justina informed him gently.

Harry looked embarrassed,

"I should address you as 'my Lord', shouldn't I?"

"Don't let it worry you," Lord Castleton said. "The angel here who brought me into the picture is Miss Mansell."

Justina could not stop her heart beating quicker as she heard Lord Castleton describe her as an angel. Then she reminded herself that he looked on her as a young girl in need of a fatherly figure.

There was a knock on the door and the Steward entered with a tray of food.

Harry's eyes lit up, but the Steward's face fell when he saw the stowaway.

"As you can see, we have a problem here," Lord Castleton said cheerfully. "I think I need to speak to the Captain. Be good enough, Chappell, to ask him to come to my cabin. I will leave Miss Mansell in charge here."

"I'll have a word with the First Officer," replied the Steward.

"You will be all right, Miss Mansell?" asked Lord Castleton.

Justina looked at Harry, tucking into the food as though it might be whipped away from him at any moment and smiled.

"We shall be fine." She brought her gaze back to the man she now believed could manage anything. "You won't let him be put off the ship, will you?"

He shook his head and gave her a reassuring smile.

"Leave it all to me. We'll sort out young Master Nicholls."

He left and Justina sat on her bed and watched Harry demolish the food.

"Feeling better?"

"Much, much better." He ran a small hand through his fair hair, now dry again and flopping over his face. "I didn't like being so dirty, Papa says a man has to keep himself clean at all times."

There was a knock at the door and Lord Castleton entered.

Harry immediately stood up.

"Have you spoken to the Captain, my Lord?"

"I have. He is waiting for you in my cabin next door."

Harry looked very apprehensive.

He shepherded the nervous boy out of the cabin.

Justina waited, as apprehensive as Harry. She tried to remember that she trusted Lord Castleton to fix everything in the best possible way.

Lord Castleton quickly returned.

"Sorry to leave you, but I thought I should introduce Harry to the Captain and not leave him to encounter the great man on his own."

He spoke cheerfully and Justina felt that things were going to be all right.

"I suppose the Captain is rather like God," she said with a smile.

"On his ship, I think you have it exactly right. Now, you will want to know what has been decided about young Master Harry."

Justina nodded eagerly.

"He is receiving a bit of a dressing down at the moment but, don't worry, the Captain is a splendid man with sons of his own. I trust him to level with Harry in just the right way. We cannot have him thinking he can ever repeat this escapade."

"I think he's been so hungry and miserable, he is not going to want to."

"I hope you are right. Now, for tonight, he will sleep in my cabin. The Steward will arrange for an extra bed. Tomorrow there are several passengers leaving the ship at Port Said, so the Captain will have an empty cabin and he is willing to allow Harry to use it for the rest of the voyage."

"My Lord, that is all your doing, I am sure," Justina sighed in heartfelt tones. "Thank you *so* much."

"No need, I am happy to be of help," murmured Lord Castleton quietly. "Now I think it is time you retired, it has been a long and exhausting day."

Justina nodded gratefully.

"You have done very well," he added. "Both with the concert and now with our stowaway. I'll see you again in the morning."

He gave her a quick smile and left.

For a long moment Justina remained where she was and savoured the glorious feeling his compliments gave her and the relief that Harry's situation had been so satisfactorily resolved.

But before she could start undressing, there was another knock at her door and Harry entered.

"I wanted to thank you for taking care of me so well and to wish you a good night," he said.

His face was glowing and he looked a different boy from the dirty rapscallion she had discovered in her cabin.

Justina hugged him, gave him a kiss and said she would see him the next day.

*

Justina woke late the next morning to find that the ship's engines had stopped.

She drew aside the curtain of her porthole to find they had docked at Port Said.

All at once the events of the previous evening flooded back into her mind and she knew that she had to ensure that Harry was being properly looked after.

The plight of the small boy who had gone through such trials in order to rejoin his family had touched her heart.

Before she could start dressing, her Stewardess appeared.

"I have a message from Lord Castleton," she said with a smile. "You are invited to lunch at Port Said. There will be a carriage waiting in an hour and will you please be ready to accompany him."

Justina gasped. It sounded wonderful, but how could she accept? There was Harry to think about and Sir Thomas.

When she thought of Sir Thomas's behaviour over the little stowaway, she decided that it would probably be best not to encounter him quite yet or she might say something she would later regret.

And as for Harry, Lord Castleton was taking care of him and he could tell her exactly what the position was.

Yes, she decided, she would accept this dazzling invitation.

Perhaps Aunt Theodora would say that she was being dangerously impulsive, but for once she did not care what the dragon Viscountess thought.

She found a light muslin shirt and skirt in a becoming shade of pale green that Dorcas had brought up the previous day beautifully ironed. There was a tie of the same muslin to arrange around the crown of her wide straw hat and a matching parasol. For once Justina thought that she was both properly and stylishly dressed.

She picked up her reticule and the parasol and left her cabin.

Almost immediately she ran into Mrs. Arbuthnot.

"Ah, my dear Justina, I was coming to find you. Such excitement, everyone is talking about our little stowaway. The girls are quite overcome with jealousy that he didn't come into our cabin last night.

"And then Lord Castleton sought me out and explained that Lord Cromer, the Governor of Egypt, has sent him an invitation to lunch. Well, not Lord Cromer himself, he, of course, is in Cairo, but his representative in Port Said, such a highly placed person, and Lord Cromer being a friend of your father's and knowing that you are also on this ship, you are included in the invitation."

Mrs. Arbuthnot drew breath and appeared to look

respectfully at Justina for the first time.

"What a pretty dress, you are quite a belle today. Well, of course, I told Lord Castleton that it would only be right if Sir Thomas attended the luncheon as well."

Justina's heart plummeted. All her anticipation evaporated. For a moment she wished Mrs. Arbuthnot had never come on the ship – almost had never been born!

Her chaperone looked slightly embarrassed as she continued,

"Lord Castleton said he was most sincerely sorry, but since the engagement has not yet been announced, it would not be possible, etiquette would not allow it. Such a shame, my dear. I do hope you do not think it is my fault you have been placed in such an unfortunate position?"

Justina tried to contain her delight.

"I am sure you did everything correctly, Mrs. Arbuthnot. Now, forgive me, but I understand that Lord Castleton has a carriage waiting and I must not be late."

"Oh, my dear, I would not delay you – "

There was more, but Justina had fled towards the gangway.

It was a busy scene on the dock.

A multitude of ships of all sizes were tied up or moving to and fro. Coaling ships were transferring fuel to steamers and the noise and bustle was tremendous.

Justina took a little time to locate Lord Castleton, but at last she saw his tall figure, elegant in cream linen, conversing with a couple of the passengers,

Justina descended onto the quayside and Lord Castleton at once came forward.

"Forgive me, I was tied up or I would have been waiting for you."

"What a lovely day it is," Justina smiled. "Mrs.

Arbuthnot tells me we are to meet Lord Cromer's representative."

She looked around but could see no one who could fit that description.

"Ah, yes, Lord Cromer's representative. Come, will you enter the carriage so we can be on our way?"

He helped Justina into the carriage. As the driver put his horse into motion, he entertained her with some details of the town.

"I should tell you that Port Said owes its origins to the existence of the Suez Canal. The port forms the northern entrance to that most convenient of modern constructions. You will know, of course, that the canal was opened in 1869. It cut the sailing time to Bombay by half. Imagine having to spend two months on board ship instead of one!"

She seemed happy to be in the carriage with him and he hoped that she would not react badly when he revealed exactly what he had arranged.

After a very short drive, the carriage reached a hotel.

Lord Castleton handed down Justina, paid off the driver and escorted her through to the restaurant.

There they were led to a table for two.

Lord Castleton allowed himself to appreciate the picture she made in her muslin dress with its wide sleeves and narrow waist. The broad hat threw a shadow over her lovely face and hid the gorgeous copper of her hair.

Justina looked around the table.

"But this is set for two, what about Lord Cromer's representative?"

"Will you be very upset if I confess that there is *no* representative? That is a tale I made up for Mrs. Arbuthnot. I was afraid that there could be trouble if I insisted we lunched together alone."

She gazed at him wide-eyed and then gave a charming little chuckle.

"You mean you lied to her?"

He nodded, keeping his expression very serious.

"I hope you will not tell Harry. It would not be a good example to set him."

Another of those charming little laughs.

"But why? I mean, why did you want to lunch with me?"

He gave a silent sigh of delight.

What other female of his acquaintance would have asked such a question? They would all have assumed that their charms were quite sufficient to elicit such an invitation.

Watson would surely at this point look deep into her eyes and say that it was because she was the most beautiful woman he knew and he wanted her all to himself.

But he was convinced that if he said anything like that, he would only embarrass her.

"I want to be able to explain what Harry's position is without the danger of interruptions from other passengers."

'Particularly Watson,' he thought.

"Oh, yes, please do tell me everything."

Across the table, Justina raised her face to look up at him. Lord Castleton enjoyed knowing that she had no idea the movement meant the inconvenient hat no longer shadowed her face.

"I have been thinking about Harry ever since you left my cabin last night," Justina began. "He needs clothes. He cannot stay the whole voyage in your shirt. Even if his things are washed, I don't think they would be very wearable."

"I have taken care of that problem. You may have seen me talking to Major and Mrs. Partridge on the quayside.

They have kindly agreed to go shopping for a new wardrobe for him. You probably know that the Partridges have very recently lost a son of Harry's age. A great tragedy that they are finding it difficult to come to terms with, so I was hesitant about asking them.

"But after I had told them Harry's story, I asked for advice on what I should get him to wear and they suggested they did the shopping themselves. Of course I was delighted as they will know exactly what he needs."

Justina's face brightened.

"That is wonderful! How tactful you are."

She paused for a moment and Lord Castleton enjoyed watching her face as it reflected so very clearly what she was thinking.

"Perhaps choosing clothes for Harry will help Mrs. Partridge feel there is still some use to life."

"I do hope so."

He reflected that as Justina revealed more and more of her character, he found his love for her becoming deeper.

Her expression remained solemn.

"I believe that not only have you organised Harry's clothes, I think you have undertaken to pay his passage."

"It is the least I could do. The poor boy has been through a nightmare. I keep thinking what if it had been a son of mine?"

"I don't think you would have sent a son of yours away like that," Justina said firmly.

"I wanted to explain all that to you. But first, I think we should order."

He steered her away from the idea of a simple salad and suggested a rice dish.

"It is always better in these parts not to eat uncooked food unless you can be completely happy with the method of its preparation," he explained.

Justina's eyes grew wide.

"Really? My goodness, that is something to remember. But is it all right on the ship? I have often eaten salad on board without any upsetting effect."

He reassured her that she could trust the ship's cooks completely.

"Now, let me explain about conditions in India. The climate there is not suited to growing children, the hot season is so very hot and there are many diseases that their constitutions find it difficult to resist. I am sure it was well explained to Harry that he must return to England for his schooling."

"Are you saying that he will have to return to England after all he has been through? That is awful!" Justina burst out.

"I am afraid almost certainly. However," he added quickly as he saw mutiny gather in her eyes, "I shall have a long talk with his parents. I am sure they will be appalled at how he has suffered. I can recommend a school where I think Harry will be happier. I have a nephew there of about the same age and I can ensure that when Harry starts, he will have him as a friend."

"If he really has to go to school in England, that sounds as though it would give him a much better chance of happiness," Justina said doubtfully.

"I am sure he will soon settle down and enjoy making other friends."

"There is also the matter of where he will spend his holidays," Justina added, still anxious. "The aunt who has been looking after him sounds dreadful. I think his parents need to find somewhere else for his holidays."

"As soon as he makes some friends, they will invite him to stay with them," he replied cheerfully. "And I am happy to have him visit me. I have already told him that he may be of help to me on the voyage by exercising Breck."

"Oh, that is too good of you," said Justina and her face lit up. "Perhaps he could come and stay with us, too."

It was the opening Lord Castleton had been hoping for.

"Us?" he asked.

"I haven't a younger brother but I am sure we can – "

Her face paled and she stopped in mid-sentence. Then her expression lost its lively quality.

"Of course, that would only be until I am married."

Justina put down her fork with a stifled sigh and the brim of her hat hid her face. She did not need to add that Harry would not be welcomed by Sir Thomas.

Lord Castleton took her hand in his.

"Justina, please, can we not admit that this ridiculous notion you are engaged to be married to Sir Thomas is a fantasy that can be quickly dismissed?"

For an instant he thought he saw hope flare into her face, but she looked straight at him and he knew he had made a serious mistake.

"Lord Castleton, pray do not talk to me in that way. Mama and Papa will be very happy that I have made such a suitable match."

"But what about *you*, Justina? Will *you* be happy?"

He saw an anguished stubbornness in her face and knew what she was going to say.

"Sir Thomas will make a good husband," she stated firmly. "Papa cannot afford to give me a large settlement so I need a well-off husband. I shall have lots of children and a very satisfying life."

"Are you sure he will make a good husband?"

Lord Castleton thought he had to push as hard as he could.

"There have been times when it seemed to me that you and he were in difficulties with your relationship."

"You have no right to talk to me in that way," Justina said in a low and furious voice. "You are not my father nor my uncle, no matter how much you think you stand in that sort of capacity. What I do with my life is for me to decide."

She stood up and snatched her reticule off the table.

"I am going back to the ship. Thank you for looking after Harry, but I do not require you to look after *me*."

She stalked out of the restaurant, followed by interested stares.

Lord Castleton swore, dropped as much money as he thought necessary on the table and hurried after her, cursing at the way he had handled the situation.

Next he found himself stopped by an old acquaintance.

Impatiently he pleaded urgent business, but when he emerged from the hotel there was no sign of Justina. Nor could he find a carriage for hire. He walked as quickly as he could back to the ship.

He needed to find her to see if he could repair the damage he had caused.

There was also the fact she had disclosed that her father's financial situation was not as good as he had thought. Did, he wondered, Sir Thomas know this?

If he told Sir Thomas and he broke the engagement, Justina might be relieved, but she would not forgive him for showing her what a poor fellow her fiancé was.

Maybe he would have saved her from disaster, but he would not have advanced his own cause.

What was he to do?

CHAPTER TEN

Justina did not find a carriage to take her back to the ship as it was not far and the tall masts in the dock meant she could hardly go wrong in finding her way.

She was so angry, she hardly noticed the heat.

How did Lord Castleton dare to talk to her so?

It did not occur to her that her anger was a way of disguising her longing for Lord Castleton to insist that her engagement to Sir Thomas was over.

Her fiancé was a handsome man and could be very charming, but Justina knew now she could never be happy with him.

She kept remembering her sister, Elizabeth, and how her initial happiness with Philip had so quickly evaporated.

As she walked, angling her parasol to ward off the sun's rays, Justina was very conscious of her bruised upper arm. Did it mean that Sir Thomas was the same kind of man as Philip? Or was it just that she had not managed yet to find the way to handle him?

Even if she was able to find out how to keep him happy, Justina knew that she would still be miserable.

It was because she loved Lord Castleton.

She recalled what her other sister, Victoria, had said about being in love. She knew she fulfilled all the conditions.

She thought about Lord Castleton all the time, he made her feel all fluttery whenever he was near and his presence made life so much brighter.

Nothing had ever been as exciting as playing the duet in the concert with him.

It was hopeless, though. Not only was she engaged to Sir Thomas, Lord Castleton was not in love with her. He thought of her as a girl who needed guidance, the daughter of a friend of his.

Her eyes filled with tears as she remembered how she had shouted at him. He had looked astonished. Which was not surprising.

Justina had never felt more miserable in her whole life.

After her rudeness to him in the restaurant, Lord Castleton would never want to speak to her again.

She found the ship and hurried up the gangway, hoping she would not meet anyone. She wanted nothing more than to find her cabin and burst into tears.

Immediately she reached the deck, however, Faith and Charity appeared. They looked immensely pleased with themselves.

"Justina!" they both shouted. "Do look, we are engaged!"

Two hands were thrust before her. Each wore a small diamond ring on the fourth finger.

"Mama is overcome with happiness," said Charity. "She thinks we have been very clever."

"And indeed *we* can announce our engagements immediately," pouted Faith. "Mama says she knows Papa will approve because Tony and Bertie are model soldiers."

"Won't you wish us happy, Justina?" gloated Charity.

"Of course," said Justina, sincerely pleased for them.

"I think you have found the best of men."

She kissed both of the girls.

"Will you do us a great favour?" asked Charity.

"If I can," said Justina, thinking that all she wanted was to get away from them. Their evident happiness only increased her misery.

"Mama insists we exercise Muffin now the noon heat has passed over, but Tony and Bertie want us to go to the Telegraph Office to send messages to their parents and to Papa," said Faith.

"Of course I will," said Justina. "I love exercising Muffin."

She meant it. The little dog had given her so many happy hours with Lord Castleton and Breck.

It would not be the same on her own, but it would still be better than collapsing in tears in her cabin.

On the upper deck she found Harry throwing a ball to Breck and frustrated squeals were coming from Muffin's kennel.

"Why," exclaimed Justina. "I see you have found something to wear."

Harry grinned at her.

"It's a bell boy's uniform. The Captain said I could wear it until something more suitable came along."

The kennel Steward came and opened up Muffin's kennel.

"Are you going to exercise a dog as well?" cried a delighted Harry. "That's great! I say, isn't Lord Castleton swell? I think he's a corker."

He threw the ball and both dogs streaked after it.

"Lord Castleton says he's going to speak to my father about my school."

157

Justina thought she had never seen such a change in anyone as in Harry. Gone was the bedraggled and miserable little boy of last night. In his place was a youngster eager to get on with life.

Breck brought the ball back and dropped it at her feet. She picked it up and threw it again. This time it was Muffin who retrieved it, catching it in her mouth after the first bounce.

"I say, isn't that dog clever!" admired Harry.

"We'd better be careful about throwing the ball too far, we don't want it to go overboard," said Justina as he threw it enthusiastically once more.

"So, Justina, this is where you have got to."

Her heart sank as she turned around.

Sir Thomas looked as angry as she had ever seen him.

"What is this I hear about you going off to lunch with Castleton?"

Justina summoned her courage.

"He said there was a special invitation – from Lord Cromer's representative – and I was asked – because of my father," she stammered.

"Don't tell me any more of your lies. One of my whist chums saw you lunching together. There was no representative of Lord Cromer or anyone else with you."

Muffin took the ball to Harry, who picked it up and stood nervously bouncing it on the deck.

"He wanted to tell me what had happened with Harry," said Justina, becoming angry herself. "There was nothing for you to get agitated about."

"So you say."

The white patches appeared again on either side of his nose.

Harry bounced the ball some more. Breck, obviously

realising that no one was going to throw it for the moment, settled down onto the deck. Muffin, though, was gazing eagerly at Harry as he rhythmically bounced the ball.

"Boy, do you have to do that?" Sir Thomas snarled, sounding even more infuriated.

Justina took a deep breath. Any minute now he would grab her by the arm in one of his punishing grips, thrust his face into hers and make some demand.

She had had enough.

"Don't talk to Harry like that," she said spiritedly.

"Don't *you* talk to me like that," he responded.

Harry was rooted to the spot throwing the ball from one hand to the other.

Justina took a deep breath. Before, though, she could say anything, Sir Thomas wrenched the ball away from Harry and threw it into the sea.

"I told you not to do that," he shouted.

Then they all watched, transfixed, as Muffin ran, jumped and sailed through the railings after the ball.

Justina screamed and ran to the side. Far below she could see the little dog thrashing around in the water.

"*Do something*!" she cried to Sir Thomas.

"Idiotic animal. Serves it right if it drowns."

"I'll fetch her," yelled Harry.

He stripped off his jacket, nimbly ducked between the railings and jumped in after the dog.

"No, Harry!" howled Justina, too late to stop him.

She looked frantically round the deck, but the Steward was not to be seen.

Breck rose to his feet and wandered over. Justina grabbed his collar.

Then she saw a lifebelt hanging on the railings. She

thrust Breck at Sir Thomas and told him to take hold of him.

Too surprised to do anything else, he hung onto the dog.

It only took Justina a moment to unfasten the lifebelt and throw it in after Harry.

It landed not far from him.

The dock was busy with small craft, but their ship was in a quiet area and no one seemed to have seen either the dog or the boy splash into the water.

Justina could see that Harry was not a good swimmer. He had managed to reach the dog, but trying to hold both the animal and grab the lifebelt was too much for him.

If help did not arrive soon, both would drown.

"You must save them," she screamed at Sir Thomas.

He paled.

"I can't swim," he wailed.

Justina looked around the deck again but there was no one in sight.

She discarded her hat and stripped off her muslin skirt and petticoat.

"Justina!" cried an outraged Sir Thomas. "What on earth are you doing?"

"Find someone to lower a lifeboat," she called as she climbed over the railing.

It seemed a long way down to the water and for a moment she hesitated. Then she remembered diving into the water with her brother from their private little cliff on holiday in Scotland. Forget the ship and the little boats, she told herself, remember how marvellous the experience was.

She lifted her arms and dived.

The water was cool after the heat on deck. She tried to keep her mouth closed as she went down and down.

At last, spluttering, she clawed her way back to the surface. Thank Heavens, she thought, that the ship had been stationary. At least she did not have far to swim to reach Harry and Muffin.

However, the water in the dock was horribly dirty. She must try very hard not to swallow any of it.

Harry was trying desperately to keep afloat without releasing the dog.

Justina looked around for the lifebelt, found it bobbing not far away and brought it to the boy.

"Give me Muffin," she gasped. "And hang onto the lifebelt. A boat will soon be here to pick us up."

She hoped desperately it would happen.

Harry seemed to want to cling onto the dog and Justina had to repeat her instructions.

At last she managed to grasp hold of Muffin and thrust the lifebelt at Harry. He looped an arm around it and finally it looked as though he was not in imminent danger of drowning.

Justina trod water and held the little dog in her arms. Muffin tried to lick her face. She was trembling and her coat was drenched.

"Are you all right, miss?" Harry managed to say.

She saw that he was using his legs to keep the lifebelt and himself near to her.

"I am fine," she called reassuringly to him. "You were wonderful to jump in after Muffin. A real hero."

"You're the hero, miss."

"Nonsense," Justina said stoutly. "I am a good swimmer. Try not to swallow any of this filthy water."

By now there were shouts coming from the ship. Passengers were appearing at the side of the main deck and waving their arms.

Then Justina saw that one of the lifeboats was swinging from its davits and appeared to be about to descend. Sir Thomas for once had done something she had asked.

Before the boat could get near the water there was a shout from the deck.

"Justina, hold on, I'm coming."

There was an enormous splash and a few moments later Lord Castleton appeared in the water beside her. A pair of strong arms enfolded her and the dog.

"My darling, what on earth did you think you were doing?" he asked.

"It's all my fault, sir – I mean, my Lord," stammered Harry.

"Don't talk," begged Justina. "This water is filthy."

The feeling of Lord Castleton's arms around her managed to be both inexpressibly comforting and exciting.

Then she said,

"Did you call me, '*darling*'?"

"Don't talk, this water is filthy," said Lord Castleton, repeating her words with a smile in his voice, but his arms tightened strongly around her. His strong legs treading the water kept them both afloat without Justina having to make any effort.

Justina was happy to let him hold her without further questions.

And now the lifeboat was in the water and two crewmen were rowing it towards them.

"Take the boy first," instructed Lord Castleton as they drew close.

A few moments later, Justina, Lord Castleton and Muffin were safely aboard and a blanket had been wrapped around each of them.

Justina, suddenly conscious that only pantaloons covered her lower limbs, was very grateful for a respectable covering.

"Where did you come from?" she asked Lord Castleton after she had thanked the crew.

"I met the Arbuthnot twins on my return to the ship and they told me you were exercising Muffin. I arrived on the upper deck to find pandemonium."

He put an arm around her, holding her close against him.

"The deck Steward was securing Breck in his kennel looking as though Armageddon had arrived and Watson was screaming something about a man overboard. I tried to get him to explain what was going on, but all he'd say was that your behaviour was inexcusable, something about a dreadful animal, and that he had told me the stowaway should have been confined to quarters."

He looked across at Harry. Despite the heat, the boy was shivering badly.

Justina thought it was probably shock more than anything else.

"Did you really jump in to save Muffin?" Lord Castleton asked Harry.

"He's an absolute hero," Justina enthused.

"If only he hadn't thrown that ball into the sea," groaned Harry, his teeth chattering.

"It was very foolish," Justina agreed and then told Lord Castleton exactly what had happened.

Next the lifeboat was back at the ship.

Cheers greeted them from the passengers watching the drama.

"Let me take Muffin," suggested Lord Castleton as the crew held the boat steady for them to step off.

At the top of the gangway stood the Captain.

"Miss Mansell, I salute you," he said. "And I apologise for the fact that the kennel Steward had taken a few moments away from his post at the critical time. He will be severely reprimanded."

"Oh, please, don't," pleaded Justina. "He has always been most helpful and I am sure he must have had something important to attend to."

"I agree," added Lord Castleton just behind her. "It was an unfortunate conjunction of events, nothing more. You are not to blame young Harry either. He is a hero too. Now, I think brandy is called for. Heaven only knows what diseases float around in that dock. Be so good as to send large tots down to both Miss Mansell's and my cabins. And we'd be grateful if someone could dry this mutt off and return her to her kennel."

The Captain clicked his fingers and a Steward appeared and took hold of Muffin.

Behind the Captain stood Dorcas, holding out Justina's dressing gown.

Justina preferred to keep the blanket around her, but she was grateful for Dorcas's presence.

"We have to talk. If you are not too exhausted, send your maid to me after you have changed," said Lord Castleton, his arm round the still shivering Harry. "Make sure she drinks the brandy," he said to Dorcas.

She nodded and led Justina towards her cabin.

Justina was exhausted. Now she was shivering as well. The over-long blanket caused her to stumble as she tried to make her way through the crowds of passengers.

A moment later, she had been swept up in strong arms and Lord Castleton was saying,

"Please, can you let us through?"

Passengers fell back as he strode to the cabins. Justina laid her head gratefully against his chest.

She could feel the beat of his heart beneath his wet clothes.

She thought she must have misheard what he had called her as he landed in the water, but she felt protected and cared for.

All too soon, they were at her cabin.

Dorcas opened the door and she was gently laid on the bed.

"Make sure those wet clothes are removed as quickly as possible," Lord Castleton ordered.

"*A bientôt,*" he added to Justina and was gone.

"What you need is a hot bath," said Dorcas. "Not that we've got anything like that here. But we have got hot water."

She helped Justina out of the wet clothes, tut-tutting about the state of the muslin shirt.

"Can't get that back into condition before India, alas."

Justina could not care less about the clothes she had felt were so flattering only a few hours ago. All she was waiting for was to see Lord Castleton again.

Dorcas worked quickly and skilfully, sponging down Justina's tired body and drying her hair as much as she could with a towel.

The brandy arrived and Justina sipped it gratefully, feeling the fiery strength travelling along her veins, bringing new life and, hopefully, something to fight the germs she must have ingested with the filthy dock waters.

Dorcas was full of gossip as she tended to Justina.

"Those Arbuthnot girls, they've managed to land their fish," she muttered as she vigorously dried Justina's bare body. "Poor lads, they never stood a chance. Not after them

165

girls realised his Lordship wasn't a bit interested in either of them."

"Dorcas, where do you hear these things?" Justina demanded, trying to comb through her tangled hair. "You've spent most of the voyage in your bunk!"

"I keeps my eyes and ears open," Dorcas replied, taking the comb out of Justina's hand and gently wielding it through the damp mass of curls.

"And something else," she added. "That Mrs. Bloxham, her maid's an old mate of mine. Anyway, as I was saying, Patty's an old comrade in arms, as you might say, and she's given me the low down on her Mistress.

"Wealthy widow she is. Last husband was a Nabob out in India. Dropped off his perch six months ago, he did, on a visit to England. Mrs. Bloxham has been taking her time getting back to India. Patty says she's looking out for a new husband, one with a bit more class than money. Bloxham apparently had the money but not the class. Anyway, Patty says she's got her eye on your Sir Thomas."

Justina said nothing.

"So I told Patty that she better look elsewhere. But Patty seemed to think Mrs. Bloxham had quite made up her mind, no matter what arrangement has already been made. And what that woman sets her mind on, she gets, so Patty says."

Justina felt a huge surge of relief. The nightmare might nearly be over.

Mama and Papa would be sorry, but Justina knew they would never want her to be unhappy, no matter how suitable the husband.

"Will you want to retire, miss?" asked Dorcas. "Or shall you want to dress again?"

"Dress, please, Dorcas."

If Lord Castleton wanted to talk to her, Justina certainly was not going to go to bed!

Quite soon, she was dressed and her hair was starting to dry. Still damp for the most part, strands were beginning to spring out in a fiery aureole around her head.

Justina felt a strange lassitude creep over her. Part of her longed for the meeting with Lord Castleton, but part of her was afraid. Afraid not only of what might transpire, but also of what might not.

Hanging over her was the fact that she was still engaged to Sir Thomas.

"Now, shall I knock on his Lordship's door and say you are ready?"

"No!"

Dorcas looked taken aback.

"No, miss?"

"I cannot talk with his Lordship now. Say – say – oh, say if he still wants to speak to me, I'll be free later."

"Very well, miss. It's not my place to question your decision of course," said Dorcas, obviously about to do just that.

Justina was so bound up in what she had to do, she had no energy left to argue with her maid.

"Quite," she said in tones of finality and left the cabin.

It took her time to find Sir Thomas. At last she tried a corner of the Promenade deck where he had several times taken her for a quiet conversation.

Sure enough, there he was – with Mrs. Bloxham, the two of them seated on deck chairs and looking as though they were perfectly comfortable with one another.

It was Mrs. Bloxham who noticed her first.

"Why, Miss Mansell! Please, come and join us. I was only saying a few moments ago to Sir Thomas how incredibly brave you were to fling off your clothes and dive into the dock after that little dog."

"It was mainly Harry I was anxious should not drown, though of course I wanted Muffin rescued as well. Mrs. Bloxham, would you think me very rude if I asked to speak to Sir Thomas alone?"

He stood glowering at her.

"I should not think of abandoning Mrs. Bloxham on her own."

"Oh, don't be ridiculous, Tom. Go along and see what your little friend wants. I shall do very well here," coaxed Mrs. Bloxham with easy familiarity.

"I shall return soon," said Sir Thomas and followed Justina round the corner. "I take it you have come to apologise," he started as soon as they were alone.

"What do you mean, apologise?"

"For your appalling behaviour in diving into the dock."

It occurred to her that he might feel guilty that he had been unable to help and that was why he reacted in this way. Whatever the reason, it provided a perfect opportunity for her to say what she had prepared.

"Sir Thomas, I see no need to apologise. Harry was drowning and he needed help. Luckily, I am a good swimmer. I knew I would be in no danger and it was natural to help."

"You exposed your legs!"

"They were clad in pantaloons, I only wish they hadn't been, they weighed me down," Justina countered belligerently.

"That is an indecent statement."

Justina looked at him steadily.

"Sir Thomas, you have paid me an enormous

compliment by asking me to be your wife."

A cautious look came into his eyes.

"But I think you now see that I am not qualified to be a suitable partner for one in your position," Justina continued. "You need someone who understands how not to offend your sensibilities and is properly aware of how to behave in all situations. I am afraid that my behaviour would cause you constant anguish."

She glanced down at the deck.

"Also, I am afraid that you could be under a misapprehension over my father's financial status. My dowry will be very small. I am sure that would not worry you, but I felt you should know."

She looked pleadingly at him.

"Our engagement has not been announced and it is simplicity itself to break it off now. I will explain my unsuitability to be your wife to my parents and they will appreciate how very understanding you have been."

Justina came to the end of her prepared speech and held her breath.

Something very much like relief came over his features.

"Justina, you have hurt me to the quick, but," he added hurriedly, "I have been feeling for some time that your physical beauty had blinded me to the fact that we do not deal well together. As you say, the engagement has been informal and there will be no blame attached to either side if it is severed."

He took a step towards her, the look she had come to dread in his eyes.

"Perhaps one last kiss?"

She backed away, grateful that there was an avenue of escape behind her.

"Sir Thomas," she said, holding up a hand. "It is better we part as friends – and remain so for the rest of the voyage. Now, I am sure that Mrs. Bloxham will be counting the moments until your return to her side."

His expression altered and a cunning look came into his eyes.

"Yes, indeed, it would be only fair to continue to keep her company. You will inform Mrs. Arbuthnot of the situation regarding our relationship?"

Justina nodded.

"And I hope she will inform Castleton," Sir Thomas continued with the hint of an underlying threat. "I would not like you to feel it was necessary to approach him on the subject."

Justina was anxious not to alienate him in any way as the interview had gone far more smoothly than she had feared.

"I am sure Mrs. Arbuthnot will do all that is required," she said.

A moment later he had returned to Mrs. Bloxham and Justina leaned against the railings feeling suddenly weak.

But her overwhelming emotion was relief. At last she was no longer tied to Sir Thomas.

All around the ship, Justina could see preparations were being made to leave the port and enter the Suez Canal. Passengers were beginning to line the sides of the ship to watch her departure.

Justina walked along the Promenade deck, looking for Mrs. Arbuthnot.

Instead, she found Harry, now dressed in a smart sailor suit and accompanied by Mrs. Partridge, who seemed much improved by having a young lad to look after.

"Miss Mansell," said Harry excitedly. "I have been

down to your cabin looking for you, I want to thank you for saving me. Mama and Papa will be so grateful."

"Thank you for jumping in after Muffin," Justina said, planting a kiss on his cheek. "My, you do look smart."

Harry looked doubtfully down at his immaculate white suit.

"It's a bit fancy. I think I preferred the uniform."

"Harry! Major and Mrs. Partridge have been very kind in choosing your new wardrobe, you need to thank them!"

"Don't worry, he's said all the right things," Mrs. Partridge smiled back at her.

The sadness was still in her eyes, but she now had an air of resolution about her that had been lacking before.

"John and I will enjoy looking after him for the rest of the voyage."

"But I will see Miss Mansell and Lord Castleton, won't I?" piped up Harry.

"You can't get away from people on board a ship, I am afraid," laughed Mrs. Partridge. "Unless you keep to your cabin, that is."

"I shall look forward to playing deck quoits with you," Justina told Harry.

"Come along, we want to see the ship sail and then it will be time to change for dinner," said Mrs. Partridge.

Justina left them hanging over the railings as crewmen prepared to release the ropes securing the ship to the quay. Already the engines were throbbing.

She was preparing to give up her search when Mrs. Arbuthnot suddenly appeared.

"Dear Justina, I have been looking everywhere for you. You and that poor little boy have saved my precious Muffin! I can never thank you enough." She brought out a lace handkerchief and dabbed carefully at her eyes.

She put the handkerchief away.

"And have you heard the wonderful news of Faith and Charity's engagements?" she asked, her face alive with delight. "My precious little girls, so happy, such lovely young men, the Colonel will be so pleased."

Justina said everything appropriate.

"And this evening Tony and Bertie will join our table. Two additional diners will be a squeeze, but we shall just have to enjoy being cosy with one another."

"There will only be six of us, Mrs. Arbuthnot," Justina intervened hurriedly. "Sir Thomas and I have agreed that we do not suit and have broken our engagement."

"Broken your engagement, Justina?" Mrs. Arbuthnot lost some of her vivacity. "Are you sure that is wise? Such a catch as Sir Thomas is?"

Justina did not want to upset the good lady, her heart was in the right place even if her mouth ran away with her.

"We should not have suited," she replied firmly. "It is fortunate that we found this out so soon. Mama and Papa and Aunt Theodora will agree. Now, should we not be changing for dinner?"

"You are right, my dear, it will not do to be late this evening of all evenings."

Justina returned to her cabin and found Dorcas waiting for her.

"Lord Castleton was that put out you disappeared without talking to him," were her first words to Justina.

Justina was dismayed.

"Did he suggest another arrangement?" she asked.

"He waited a good half hour for you and then I heard him leave his cabin."

Without any message for her!

Justina's heart sank.

She had sorted out one problem, but in the process had alienated the most important person in the world.

"I have got this gown ready for you, miss. I hope you will approve."

"Anything will do," Justina said listlessly.

Justina might not care how she looked, but Dorcas considered it her duty to turn out her Mistress in the first rank of fashion.

By the time she had finished, Justina was a vision in the white lace dress, her copper hair beautifully arranged on top of her head with curly wisps artfully framing her face.

*

The Arbuthnot table was merry, Faith and Charity laughing and joking with their fiancés, Mrs. Arbuthnot ordering champagne and going into ecstatic accounts of her plans for a joint wedding.

Mrs. Bloxham was sitting at Sir Thomas's table. Justina bowed to them as she took her place with the Arbuthnots and received a gracious acknowledgement.

It took a little time before Justina could bring herself to look towards Lord Castleton's table.

He sat, as usual, by himself, studying papers. However, he took longer than usual to eat his meal and sat drinking a glass of wine after he had finished.

Justina had to force herself not to look in his direction. She did, however notice him leave. He took a route out of the Saloon that did not pass their table.

Justina felt an overwhelming depression. She had offended him. He did not want to talk to her now.

The Head Steward appeared at the table followed by another Steward holding an ice bucket containing a bottle of champagne.

"With Lord Castleton's compliments to the Misses Arbuthnot," he proclaimed.

"How very kind," Mrs. Arbuthnot gushed. "What a shame he is no longer in the Saloon so that we can thank him. But we shall find him later."

The Head Steward issued instructions for the champagne to be poured.

During this operation, Justina found that a folded piece of paper had been unobtrusively slipped beneath her side plate.

When she glanced up at the Head Steward in surprise, he gave her the tiniest of nods together with a complicit smile.

No one else at the table seemed to have noticed anything.

She carefully and secretly placed it in her reticule.

A feeling of great excitement filled her. It must be from Lord Castleton.

After a little, she excused herself saying that she was exhausted.

No one seemed surprised and good wishes followed her out of the Saloon.

Once outside, she read the message.

"I shall be on the upper deck and hope that you will be able to join me there."

It was signed with a large 'C'.

For a moment Justina stood and looked at it. Excitement coursed through her. Lord Castleton *did* want to see her.

Then reason took over. She had abandoned him in a public restaurant and made him look a fool. Then he had been forced to dive into a filthy dock to rescue her.

Of course he wanted to see her – and in a private place

that was not a cabin where someone could invade their privacy and compromise both him and her.

All the excitement drained away.

Well, she had better get it over with.

Justina carefully folded up the note and replaced it in her reticule. After the voyage was over, she would at least have it to remember him by.

Slowly she mounted the companionway to the upper deck.

Despite her conviction that nothing pleasant awaited her at the top, Justina found her steps quickening as she reached the small landing that led out onto the deck.

Nervously she opened the door and stepped outside.

The night was softly warm, the air caressing as the ship steamed along the Canal in darkness. The sky above was studded with stars, the moon silvered the narrow stretch of water they were travelling along.

Light from the ship's living areas dimly lit the deck and Justina could make out the kennels where Breck and Muffin would now be safely asleep.

Beyond, standing by the railings and looking out at the bare banks of the canal was the tall, aristocratic figure of Lord Castleton.

He turned as soon as Justina started across the deck towards him.

"You came," he said and she recognised relief in his tone.

It gave her courage.

"I was surprised to receive your note as I thought you had decided I did not want to speak to you."

"But you do?"

"It was very rude of me to leave you like that at the restaurant this afternoon, I want to apologise, my Lord."

"Oh, do stop calling me that. My name is Marcus."

Justina thought it suited him perfectly.

"And also my – Marcus, I want to thank you for jumping into the water to save Harry and me. And Muffin," she added scrupulously.

"Have you seen Harry?"

She nodded.

"He is fine and Mrs. Patridge seems to be enjoying looking after him."

"She and her husband returned from shopping in Port Said with a whole retinue of shop assistants carrying parcels."

There was an underlying humour in his voice that allowed Justina to relax slightly.

Being so close to him was a dizzying experience.

She could feel every breath he drew and was conscious of his nearness in a way that made her shiver, despite the warmth of the night air.

She knew that she would never love anyone else with the intensity that she loved him.

He moved slightly towards her, leaving only a small gap between them. He peered at her face as though he would discern her expression by the light of the moon.

"You accused me at lunch of behaving like an uncle or surrogate father," he said abruptly, speaking very fast. "That is not the case. My feelings towards you are not at all avuncular nor paternal."

It took a moment for Justina to understand what he was saying and then she gave a little gasp.

"You have placed me in a damnable position with your unacknowledged engagement – knowing what I know and believing what I believe."

Justina felt a joy such as she had never experienced

begin to flood through her. Surely she could not misinterpret his words?

"Which is what, *Marcus*?"

It was sheer delight just to speak his name and feel his hands grip hers tightly.

"To know that this engagement is all wrong for you and not to be able to tell you what I feel."

"What do you feel, Marcus?"

She was unable to resist saying his name again.

She could sense his sudden stillness as he took in her intimate, caressing tone.

"Do I understand that you are no longer engaged to Thomas Watson?"

His voice trembled as though he wanted it so much to be true, he hardly dared to believe it.

"We have agreed that we would not suit. That is why – " her voice, too, trembled. "That is why I could not meet you earlier."

"What are you saying?"

"I knew that before I saw you again, I had to be free."

"And you are!" he said triumphantly. "And you feel as I feel!"

"How do you feel, Marcus?"

Justina had to hear him say it even though every fibre of her being was telling her that what she had longed for so desperately was coming true.

"That I love you as I never dreamed I could love. That you have brought me to life again and I cannot face the desolation of what my existence would be without you at my side," he said, the words tumbling over themselves.

"I know you adored your late wife and I know I can never take her place."

He put his finger over her lips.

"Shhh, no more. Somewhere Ariadne is smiling her approval of what is happening. Our relationship was very special, but it is in the past. *You* are my present and my future."

He drew her into his arms and held her tight.

"Ever since I first saw you defending that damn mutt Muffin, you captured my heart. I knew that you were the only one for me."

His hand gently raised her chin so that the moonlight fell full on her face.

"My darling, you are the most beautiful woman in the world and also the kindest, most loyal and most fun. *I love you*. I want you to marry me and make me the happiest man in the world."

Then his head came down and his mouth fastened on hers.

Justina felt her soul rise in her body.

Unimaginable sensation filled her as she responded to his kiss. It was so different from the times Sir Thomas had kissed her.

This was what love was like.

It was as though their bodies had become one and risen to the Heavens above.

If she held out her hand, she would be able to touch the stars that spangled the night's velvet.

Heavenly joy was hers and life could begin.